# PAWSITIVELY YOURS FOR CHRISTMAS

## CHRISTMAS IN SNOWY FALLS BOOK 3

JACQUELINE WINTERS

Copy Editor: Write Girl Editing Services

Cover Design: Blue Valley Author Services

Proofreading: FictionEdit.com

## CHAPTER 1

ILL

Will Taggert loved this time of year in Snowy Falls. He strolled downtown as light, puffy snowflakes cascaded so slowly from the sky they might as well have been floating. Giant wreaths with sparkly red bows hung from old-fashioned light poles. Frosty window fronts twinkled with Christmas lights, highlighting unique holiday displays. It felt as though he were walking through a snow globe.

Every person he passed greeted him warmly, asking if he'd finished his Christmas shopping—*no, he hadn't*—or if he was driving the fire truck for the Christmas Eve parade that preceded the annual tree lighting ceremony—*yes, he was*—and most often where his trusty four-legged sidekick, Grimm, was. The pair was rarely seen apart.

"I'm headed to pick him up from Tail Waggers right now," he explained to the third person who asked.

"That reminds me," Mrs. Dabney said, patting her purse. "I better give your sister a call. See if she can't fit in my Waffles before Christmas."

"Better call soon." When Libby Taggert opened her dog grooming salon two years ago, he worried the small Maine town wouldn't be able to support her business. But to his welcome surprise, her days were often booked solid. He'd begged her to squeeze in Grimm last minute, promising next time he'd heed her advice and schedule the requested two weeks in advance. "Might bribe her with some of your famous Santa's whiskers cookies," he added as an afterthought.

Mrs. Dabney winked at him before they went their separate ways.

Standing across the street from Tail Waggers, Will noticed a cloud of fog in the salon's storefront window. A giant nose pressed against the glass in the center of it. The pointed tips of familiar ears poked out at the top of the fog circle as Will waited for a car to pass before crossing. Grimm was one of the only dogs Libby allowed to roam freely in the shop, probably because most of Snowy Falls residents knew the Great Dane and loved him.

His heart swelled in gratitude as it often did when he recalled how Grimm had come into his life. The eldest Taggert sister, Chloe, found the pup five years ago—cold, abandoned, and severely malnourished in a Portland park. She'd taken him home and nursed him back to health. Though she waited the allotted time for his owner to claim him, she already knew he was meant for Will.

He couldn't imagine his life without the giant, lovable goofball.

Will barely made it inside the salon before Grimm charged toward the entrance, greeting him with eager kisses to the cheeks. The dog was the size of a small horse on all fours. But when he jumped and posted two paws on Will's shoulders, he became a giant. "Grimm, aren't you a handsome boy? You even *smell* like Christmas."

"Roasted chestnut, to be precise," Libby explained as she fixed a display of doggie Christmas toys Grimm knocked over with his eager, whipping tail. The thing could be wielded as a weapon, though the Great Dane would never harm a fly on purpose. Sweet Grimm loved everyone. *Well, almost everyone.*

Grimm lowered to all fours and plopped his bottom on the floor, proudly showing off his new bandana. "Red with candy canes. Nice touch."

"Thought it checked off the right boxes for tomorrow—Christmas themed and fire-engine red." Libby handed Will the leash, and he clipped it on. If he wasn't mistaken, there was dog shampoo bubbles in her hair.

"Hope he behaved for you," Will said as Grimm trotted beside him to the counter.

"He was a good boy today." Libby brushed a hand over her dark green apron adorned in Christmas stockings and pawprints, but it did little to remove the blanket of dog hair stuck to it. "Except for some dramatics when I trimmed his nails."

Grimm shoved his head under Will's hand, demanding sympathy, no doubt for the exploitation. Or maybe it was to remind his owner he hadn't given him a treat yet. A plastic container decorated in Christmas and paw prints stickers sat on the edge of the counter, and Grimm kept sneaking looks at the peanut butter biscuits inside it.

"Still working on that, huh, boy?"

"I'm surprised you didn't hear him crying down at the fire station." Libby flipped through an open binder on the counter, skimming one column with her finger. "At least he didn't try to bite—or should I say *destroy*—the dryer this time."

Grimm looked up at Will with those big brown doe eyes that melted his heart every time. He relented and fished a bone-shaped morsel from the container. "Don't worry," he whispered to the dog as Libby took a phone call. "I won't tell the third graders about this if you don't."

He waited for his sister to scribble an appointment in her notebook and end the call. Libby looked worn out, but that sparkle still twinkled in her eyes. Though she was doing what she loved, he couldn't help but wonder if she felt something was missing. "I could earn a year's wages the week before Christmas. All I'd have to do is forfeit sleep and book appointments twenty-four hours a day."

"Speaking of, how much do I owe you?" Will pulled his wallet from his interior jacket pocket as another dog barked from the back. He was surprised Libby still had another client tonight, late as it was.

"Bowzer's just drying off," Libby said before he could ask whether she'd given more thought to hiring help. "He'll be going home within the hour."

Will handed over his card.

Libby refused it. "Merry Christmas."

"Does this count as my gift this year?" he teased, stuffing it back into his wallet. Will thought the whole gift-giving thing was excessive, especially for his family of nine—eleven this Christmas since the past year had included two weddings. But every year he suggested drawing names, his siblings gave him death glares. Especially his three sisters.

Libby rolled her eyes in response. "Knock it off."

Will put his hands up in surrender. "Okay, okay. You win."

She pinned him in place with a laser-beam stare. "You haven't even started your Christmas shopping, have you?"

"Christmas is still five days away." Never mind that they'd all be exchanging gifts after the Christmas Eve feast at Grandma Annie's. Which meant he in fact only had four days to procure all those gifts. "Plus, Lane and Cole are in Ireland this year."

"I'm surprised you didn't go with them."

The phone rang again, saving him from an explanation.

Will had been invited, but the thought of spending Christmas away from Janie was reason enough to turn down the trip. This was the first holiday in as many as he could remember that his best friend was single. Maybe this Christmas would be the one he confessed his true feelings. He couldn't do that very well from Ireland.

"You still have to buy them gifts," Libby said firmly when she finished the call.

"I will, I will," he promised, thankful at least that his best friend would wrap them. He'd been swamped with annual inspection paperwork at the fire station all day and hadn't talked to her yet. He reached for his phone with the intention of sending Janie a quick text, bribing her with her favorite gingersnap cookies in exchange for her expert giftwrapping services. But Libby interrupted him before he could unlock the screen.

"You bringing a date this year?"

"This question gets old," Will grumbled.

"Oh, wait—all you need is Grimm, *right?*"

"Right." It was easier to pretend he preferred the bachelor life than admit he'd been pining after the same woman for an embarrassing number of years. When Libby seemed about to press, he interjected. "Are *you* bringing a date?"

"Touché."

He'd been in love with Janie Arden since the sixth grade, but she'd never seen him as more than a friend. It didn't help that every Christmas she had some boyfriend or another. The silver lining was that none of them seemed to stick. "I better be going," he said, his growling stomach reminding him he hadn't eaten since lunch. He could swing by his parents' place in search of leftovers. Mom was an amazing cook all year round, but during the holidays she went all out. Or he could stop by The Twisted Lobster to see if Janie was working at her parents' restaurant tonight.

"You heading to the city council meeting?" Libby asked.

"Wasn't planning on it," he answered. "Why, should I go?"

She shrugged. "Might not hurt to make an appearance from time to time. You do still want that deputy fire chief position when it opens someday, right?"

If the rumors were true, that day might be sooner rather than later. "Good point."

Bowzer let out a series of impatient barks. "That's my cue."

Will held the door open for Grimm, who began biting at falling snowflakes the moment his head poked outside. He *should* go to the city council meeting if he wanted a future in Snowy Falls. He loved this small town. Had grown up here and only left for the two years he and Janie attended community college. He couldn't imagine living anywhere else.

Except Janie was dead set on ending up in Boston.

If he could ever convince her to take a chance on them as more than friends, he'd have to wrap his head around a long-distance relationship. He couldn't imagine ever *living* in Boston. Life would be too different in a busy city. For him *and* for Grimm. No, Snowy Falls was their home.

At the intersection, Will looked longingly down the block toward The Twisted Lobster. Despite the heavy temptation of Maine's best seafood alfredo and a chance to see Janie, Will turned and crossed the street toward city hall instead.

"There you are!" Janie grabbed onto his arm, using it to slow her shuffling feet. She nearly slipped on a patch of ice. Grimm let out a deep bark as Will caught her in time, helping her find her footing. His heart warmed from the inside out at her unexpected appearance. "Don't you check your phone?" she demanded, scrubbing a mitten-clad hand behind Grimm's long neck.

"Haven't had a chance yet—"

"You're coming with me." Both arms looped through his, she tugged him down the block with more force than the eager dog. "I'm not going to this city council meeting alone."

"Wait, why are *you* going?"

"Dad sent me to make sure the sidewalk dining ordinance gets passed." Will tried to recall the conversation about this, but he was too distracted by the way Janie remained latched to him as they headed toward City Hall. "Don't have a clue why they're discussing it in December," she added in a mutter. "This is what I get for being single. They think I have all the time in the world."

Will couldn't help the smile that formed across his lips. It felt like a sign.

"But I'm sticking to it this year."

"Sticking to what?"

"I'm staying single, Will. I mean it this time. I keep putting my dreams second to some relationship that fizzles out right after the holidays." Janie released his arm as they turned the last corner and followed the crowd toward the City Hall entrance. Grimm's ears perked, no doubt at the prospect of all the friendly pats. "I'm tired of planning small-town birthday parties and baby showers in between all the obligations involved with dating someone."

"You make it sound exhausting." Will hoped he hid his disappointment effectively behind shaky laughter.

"It *is* exhausting. That's why I'm swearing off dating until my event planning business is off the ground. All I want for Christmas this year is a real chance to bring my dream to life."

Will forced a smile for the benefit of Janie and everyone around them, though inside his heart squeezed in defeat. All *he* wanted for Christmas was for his best friend since the sixth grade to fall in love with him.

## CHAPTER 2

ANIE

Janie Arden wished she were anywhere else aside from the monotonous Snowy Falls city council meeting. Binders, photos, and craft supplies were strewn all over her living room, beckoning her attention. If she wanted to get her event planning business off the ground, she needed those portfolios assembled and looking their best.

Grimm dropped his head in her lap, letting out a groan. At least she wasn't here alone. "I know," she whispered to the dog. "I'm as bored as you are."

For years, Janie had planned anniversary, graduation, and retirement parties in between her shifts at the family restaurant. Sometimes she even arranged holiday office parties. She was *good* at it. She had an eye for small details that often brought happy tears to the eyes of her clients. But she was ready for bigger challenges. Galas, awards banquets, and charity dinners. Events grander than little Snowy Falls could accommodate.

"Did you know that Erin Carlile is planning *the* New Year's Eve gala this year?" she whispered to Will as the council called on citizens to express their thoughts and concerns about a crosswalk signal at the busiest downtown intersection. Erin Carlile was Janie's event planner idol. Janie stalked her career— online, of course—and read every review of her work. She had an entire notebook filled with tips, notes, and takeaways from blogs and interviews. If she had a Christmas wish this year, it'd be to attend one of Erin Carlile's events and meet the queen of event planning herself. But invites, much less tickets, were nearly impossible to come by.

"The one in Boston?"

"Yeah."

"We should go."

Janie let out a laugh that she was forced to turn into a cough to keep from disrupting the meeting. "It's a formal event," she whispered to Will after the attention was no longer on her.

"So?"

"You in a suit?" She stared up at him, certain he

was teasing. "I can't picture it. Besides, the event is sold out." She was always a day late when it came to the possibility of attending one of Erin's events. A detail she typically discovered while listening to the radio as the station gave away the *last* tickets to the event. She'd never been the lucky caller. Seemed you had to know someone to procure tickets at all.

It was just as well. She was determined to stick to her resolve this year and avoid dating to focus on her own business. And she'd need a date to attend an event like that. Will's offer was made simply in kindness of their years-long friendship. He'd hate every minute of a fancy gala. Janie would never let him put himself through that kind of torture, even if she was lucky enough to score tickets.

As the meeting droned on, Janie flipped through her planner. Despite her eagerness to move on to bigger and fancier events, she still had three parties to put together right after Christmas. She ran through her checklists for each, not surprised to discover that most of the arrangements and to-do items were complete. She'd become a well-oiled machine when it came to planning small-town parties. It was why she craved something more that would challenge her.

Will leaned against her shoulder and whispered, "They're talking about your sidewalk dining ordinance."

Janie flipped to a lined page in the back of her

planner and prepared to take notes. She'd squabbled with her parents about attending the city council meeting, convinced that her presence wouldn't change the outcome of the council's decision regarding local restaurants using public sidewalks outside their restaurants for summer diners. A decision everyone expected the council to rule in favor of anyway.

But Mom and Dad were scrambling to fill a last-minute catering request—one their barely in-the-black restaurant needed right now. Janie could never tell them no, even if she pretended she wanted to.

"Does anyone have any last comments about this ordinance before we make a motion to approve?" Lynette Jergensen asked the room.

Janie glanced around the room but didn't see a single person raise their hand. As she thought, the ordinance passed without issue. She stuffed her planner into her tote bag and zipped up her coat.

"You leaving?" Will asked, eyebrows drawn in confusion.

"Are you staying?"

He leaned over and lowered his voice. "The chief's here."

Janie followed his nod three rows ahead and a few seats to the left. Fire Chief Gundersen was hard to miss with his broad shoulders and tall frame. She pitied the couple sitting behind him as it was doubtful they could see the stage. Though she yearned to get home, she wouldn't abandon Will. If rumors held true, the deputy fire chief position would be open within the next year, and no one deserved it more than Will.

Grimm thumped his tail against the chair leg when she unzipped her coat. She'd always wanted a dog, but if she was going to move to Boston in the near future, getting one wouldn't be fair or practical. At least Boston was only little more than an hour away and she could always visit Grimm.

"We have one last matter on the agenda to discuss," Lynette announced.

Janie breathed a quiet sigh of relief that the meeting was nearly over. The sooner they got out of here, the sooner she could grab a lobster mac and cheese to-go plate while updating her parents, and then spend the rest of her night finishing her portfolio binders.

"As most of you are aware, Snowy Falls is hosting a Christmas Eve charity event in this building." Something about Lynette's tone hooked Janie's attention, and she sat up straighter in her chair. "Unfortunately, the event planner we had lined up was in Vermont this past weekend and suffered some broken ribs and a broken leg from a skiing accident. She's canceled on us."

Janie's heart raced, sensing opportunity.

"We need to vote whether to cancel the event or to find someone who can fill in last minute. Many of the details are arranged, but it's still quite an under-taking for someone new to take over this close to Christmas Eve."

Janie bolted upright out of her chair before Lynette could put the matter to a vote. "I can do it." The words were out before she had time to consider the gravity of their meaning. She'd seen the flyers around town the for the charity dinner event to be held on Christmas Eve before the parade and tree lighting ceremony. But she had no idea what was all involved in an event the town had never hosted.

"Janie Arden, are you volunteering to take over the event?" Lynette asked.

"I am."

Will tugged on the edge of her jacket until she finally glanced back at him. "What are you doing?"

"Seizing an opportunity," she answered through gritted teeth as chatter erupted at the council table. Grimm licked her wrist, whether in support or sympathy, she wasn't certain. She ran her fingers softly behind his ears, holding her ground.

"Janie—"

"Do we have any other volunteers or suggestions for an event planner replacement?" Lynette asked the room. She was met with resounding silence. Janie's palms grew slightly sweaty. Snowy Falls didn't have an official event planner. No one local wanted to take over planning such a massive town event four days out. That had to be the reason she had no competition.

The council murmured amongst themselves.

Janie looked back at Will, relieved to see a half smile curled on his lips. It was a smile that single women loved to talk about in local coffee shops and yoga classes. Will Taggert could have any woman in Snowy Falls he wanted, but Janie couldn't recall the last time he had a girlfriend.

"You're sure?" Will asked her in that familiar tone that helped ground her but also promised support. She was lucky to have him as a friend.

She gave him a nonchalant shrug, pretending the complete lack of Christmas décor in the auditorium didn't jump out at her like a sore thumb. Decorations were nothing. This close to Christmas Eve, the event was likely organized. And whatever details still needed sorting, well, those might lend to that challenge she sought. "How hard could it be?"

"We're going to put the matter to a vote," Lynette announced, pulling Janie's attention back to the front of the auditorium. "The vote is whether to have Janie Arden take over planning of the Christmas Eve charity event or to cancel it altogether."

Janie convinced herself the outcome didn't matter. Even if the citizens in attendance voted to cancel the event, at least she'd been brave enough to step up and offer her services. If they voted in her favor, she could add something bigger than birthday parties and bridal showers to her portfolio. It could take her one step closer to achieving her dream.

"All those in favor of Janie Arden taking over as the event planner?"

Hands shot up across the room in a wave, including Will's. Grimm let out a deep bark that echoed off the high ceilings and won him some laughter. Janie's heart swelled with gratitude at the support of the Snowy Falls community.

"All those in favor of canceling the event?"

Two hands meekly lifted into the air, but Janie was too excited to pay attention to her opposition. She'd prove them wrong, whomever they were.

"Janie Arden," Lynette announced, "it looks like you'll be heading the First Annual Snowy Falls Christmas Eve Charity Event."

## CHAPTER 3

ILL

"And what do we do when we go to bed?" Will asked the roomful of eager-eyed third graders.

Half a dozen hands shot up into the air. He wasn't sure whether their rapt attention to his Christmas tree safety presentation was because he wore his firefighter uniform or if Grimm had stolen the show with his goofy expression and proud display of his red candy cane bandana. He liked to think it was a team effort.

Will called on a girl with pigtails in the second row. "Turn out the lights!"

"Yes, turn out the lights. Very good." Grimm barked in agreement, eliciting a classroom full of laughter. Including the teacher, Ms. Alicia Meadows. When he told Janie last night whose classroom he'd be visiting, she suggested he ask Alicia to be his date for the Christmas Eve charity event, confirming Janie really was clueless about his true feelings for her. "Are there any other safety tips we haven't covered?"

The various expressions of concentration made it hard not to laugh. Kids were so animated and entertaining, especially when they weren't trying to be. At twenty-five, he thought he'd already be married. Have at least one kid on the way. But he hadn't expected to still be hung up on Janie *and* stuck in the friend zone. He caught Ms. Meadows' gaze and wondered if it was time to give up this endless pining for Janie and move on. Even if it was, he wasn't sure he could do it.

"Anyone?" he asked again.

Will gave Grimm the signal, and the dog popped up to all fours. Ears perked, tail wagging, tongue hanging out the side of his mouth, he scanned the room like Will taught him when he was the clue.

A little boy in the third row shot his hand into the air, waving it impatiently until Will called on him. "Make sure your dog doesn't drink the tree water!"

Grimm's deep bark echoed in the classroom. "Right. If you have pets, you'll want to keep an eye on the water level. You don't want your Christmas tree to dry out and become a fire hazard because your dog or cat got thirsty and helped themselves."

"Does Grimm drink Christmas tree water?" a girl asked.

"No, he's a very good boy. He takes fire safety very seriously." Hard to drink tree water when Will hadn't even put one up. Most holidays, he never got around to getting a tree, much less decorating one. This year, however, he had a plan. "Any other questions?"

Hands shot up in the air and waved around. He called on every kid, unsurprised that many of their questions were unrelated to Christmas tree fire safety. Most were about Grimm and what tricks he could do.

When the bell rang announcing recess, Will and Grimm made their escape before things grew awkward with Ms. Meadows. She was a lovely woman with a generous heart and kind smile. A real catch.

But she wasn't Janie.

———

"This is perfect," Chloe said as Will dropped a pile of retired fire hose on a pallet outside the former garage that'd been converted into a kennel. Barking erupted from inside as Grimm and his sister's dog,

Belle, raced around the fenced-in yard. "I can make at least twenty toys out of these."

"Sounds like you have some new rescues?" Will nodded toward the kennel.

"Three, actually. Boomer, Shadow, and George."

"George?"

"If you met him, you'd get it." Chloe's eyes sparkled, much the way Libby's did at the grooming salon last night. She'd been running her side business, Chloe's K9 Creations, for a few years. Her homemade treats, beds, blankets, and toys were available in several smaller Maine towns she frequented on her runs to pick up rescues. Lately, business was picking up in big ways.

"Heard you've been getting a lot of donations," Will mentioned.

"Yes, so many. Will, I think in a year or two, Parker and I could do this full time." She gripped his sleeve enthusiastically. "Think of how many dogs we could help!"

At the mention of his brother-in-law, Will was reminded of the Christmas shopping he still needed to do. Thankfully Janie was meeting him shortly to help. But even she might have trouble figuring out what to give the newest member of the family. "Parker a football fan or anything like that?"

Chloe raised a knowing eyebrow at him. "You haven't started your Christmas shopping yet, have you?"

"I'm about to."

"Janie saving your bacon again this year?" Chloe's eyes sparkled with an entirely different kind of emotion—mischief. His family loved Janie and welcomed her with open arms anytime she joined in on family functions. But Chloe seemed the biggest threat to discovering his secret feelings for her.

"She's better at this whole gift thing."

Belle raced up to Chloe and dropped a slobbery tennis ball at her feet. Grimm eyed it eagerly. Chloe picked it up and chucked it, watching both dogs race after it. "I heard she's single. *Before* Christmas."

"Knock it off, Chloe."

"Oh, come on." She let out an exasperated sigh. "Tell me you haven't at least *thought* about bringing her as your date to Grandma Annie's Christmas Eve feast?"

He'd thought of nothing else, especially this year. Bringing a date to his grandma's was a big deal. Something no one dared to do unless they were serious. Well, except for Blakely. She tended to invite the only people Grimm didn't like. "Mind watching Grimm?" he asked, hoping to move the subject away from his pitiful prospects with Janie.

"You meeting Janie?" She wriggled her eyebrows at him.

*Well, that failed.* "I need to get Christmas shopping done, and Grimm's too big for most of the stores." Though the lovable Great Dane was welcomed in most places in town even when other dogs weren't, Will never brought him into the gift shops. There wasn't enough aisle room in the tight, centuries-old buildings. His tail alone could ring up a hundred-dollar charge in three seconds flat.

"I'll watch Grimm," Chloe relented.

He suspected a *but* was coming and made his exit before she could voice it. "Thank you," he called, hurrying to his truck. "Be back in a couple hours."

"Don't forget about Lane and Cole," Chloe hollered after him. "Just because they're in Ireland—"

Will hopped in the truck and drove off, waving at his sister. He loved his family, even for all their opinions and occasional meddling. He was blessed to have siblings he could always count on and parents who set a picture-perfect example of a strong marriage. He wanted that someday. *Preferably with Janie.*

He parked the truck near the fire station since the main strip was filled with cars—*ha*, he wasn't the only one doing last-minute Christmas shopping—and walked the block and a half to The Maine Bean to meet Janie. She refused to function without coffee. It made her the only easy person in his life to shop for around the holidays. He'd special ordered an array of unique Christmas coffee flavors made in Connecticut. The package delivery notification on his phone promised he'd ordered the gift in the nick of time.

"You're late." Janie held out a coffee to him before he could get all the way in the door. Just as well since the coffee shop was packed. She waited for him to take the cup then looped her free arm with his. "Lucky for you, I know what kind of coffee you like."

Will pretended to cautiously taste the beverage, secretly thrilled that she remembered his favorite holiday coffee. "Peppermint latte. You're good."

"I remember the little details," Janie said, leading them two doors down to the first gift shop, of which he hoped were *not* many. He held the door open for her. "That's what makes me so good at my job. No, job isn't the right word." Inside the shop, she bit the corner of her lip and looked absently at the tin antique ceiling. "Career. That's what it's going to be after this Christmas Eve charity event. A full-blown career."

"Everything going smoothly then?" he asked as he followed her through the store. "With taking that over?"

"Pretty much. I need a strategy to sell the rest of the tickets, though. What I wouldn't give to pick Erin Carlile's brain. She'd know exactly what to do." She studied a display of soft, fuzzy scarves. She unfolded one that was three different shades of blue and nodded in approval before handing it to him. "For

Libby. Her favorite color is blue. See? I *remember* these things. You should try it in case I don't make it home for Christmas one year. You know, when my event planning business explodes in Boston."

"I couldn't do this without you," Will admitted, pretending his heart didn't squeeze painfully at the thought of her moving away. It was only little more than an hour's drive on a good day, but it might as well be another world. Friendly small town versus bustling city. "Or wrapping gifts. I'm *terrible* at that."

Janie pinned him with a narrowed stare. "I taught you how to wrap last year."

"And I'm only slightly *less* terrible at it."

"I think you're faking," she accused, setting her coffee cup on a shelf so she could pick up a hand-crafted snowman with both hands. "You just don't like how much time it takes to do it right."

Will could wrap presents if he really put his mind to it. He supposed anyone could. But if he *didn't* put his mind to it, Janie would feel obligated to save the day. Considering he always provided her favorite gingersnaps, he considered it a win-win.

This year, more than any other, he longed to spend as much time with her as possible. He'd never get in the way of Janie pursuing her dreams. But he made a hard decision on the way home last night. He wasn't going to let her leave for Boston without being honest. This was the Christmas he was going to tell Janie Arden how he really felt, even if it meant losing her forever. He had to know whether or not it was time to move on.

"I guess I could make time to wrap my own presents," he said tucking the snowman—for Mom, of course—into the crook of his arm. "Though something else will have to give. Who needs a tree anyway?"

Janie spun around at him so quickly he nearly ran her over. "You don't have a tree yet?"

Will shrugged nonchalantly, fighting the laughter bubbling inside. Most years he didn't have a tree, but she was always too preoccupied with whatever boyfriend she was dating to notice. Her expression, a combination of mortified and shocked, was adorable. One he yearned to be privy to for the rest of their lives. "I've been busy. And now that I have all these presents to wrap—"

"You're impossible, Will Taggert." Janie took a generous gulp of her latte. "Okay," she added after a deep inhale and exhale. "I'm coming over tonight and we're decorating your tree. This whole anti-holiday-spirit thing in your house stops *this* year or I'm siccing your mother on you."

Robyn Taggert was about the biggest fan of Christmas he knew. Janie knew it, too. Which meant his plan was working perfectly. He'd order some lobster mac and cheese from her parents' restaurant and pick up Janie's favorite mint chocolate pie for dessert. She wasn't the only one who remembered the little things. "One thing," he said.

"Don't tell me your whole family is flying to Cancun again."

A goofy smile spread across his lips as he studied her expression. "If you hadn't spent your holiday season last year preoccupied with that dentist from Portland, you could've been on a beach too."

"Don't remind me," she mumbled.

"Wait, you *missed* me last year, didn't you?"

She threw a pair of handmade gloves at him, hitting his chin before they dropped into his arms. "Of course, I missed you." His heart leapt in his chest. "I had to carry all those Christmas decorations for the Hoffman, Hoffman, and Olivander holiday party by myself. The elevator was out, and I had to lug everything up *three* flights of stairs."

"Rest assured the Taggert clan is not going anywhere this year, aside from Cole and Lane who are already gone." Will carried his purchases to the counter and handed over his credit card. He'd been so focused on his plan to win over Janie that he had no clue how many presents they still needed to find. "But I still need to *get* a Christmas tree if I'm going to decorate one."

Janie shook her head. "Can't say I'm surprised."

"I'm so lucky you put up with me."

"You have no idea." She dug her phone out of her purse, her playful expression dropping.

"What is it?"

"My Santa canceled." Biting down on the side of her lower lip, she looked at him with a devious twinkle in her eyes. "*You* could play Santa."

"What? Oh no, I can't—"

"How badly do you want my help wrapping gifts?"

"We offer gift wrapping," the store clerk chimed in, though never in a million years would Will have taken him up on it. Every minute he could carve out with Janie was crucial. But it was certainly fun to let her *think* he'd accept the offer.

"Oh, really?"

"He doesn't need gift wrapping," Janie interjected with a forced smile, feigning sweetness. He wondered how many of her old boyfriends saw through those smiles and appreciated the feistiness beneath them. "Laugh all you want, Will Taggert. But if you want another minute of my time, you're filling in for Santa on Christmas Eve."

He'd have to work out something with the chief if it conflicted with his driving the fire truck for the parade, but he wasn't going to let Janie down. He only hoped when Christmas was all said and done, she didn't let *him* down with a broken heart.

## CHAPTER 4

*J*ANIE

"You can't hang two green ornaments so close together," Janie said, taking the metal ball from Will before he could successfully place it three inches from another just like it. He'd successfully conned her into helping decorate the tree tonight by agreeing to be Santa for the charity event. But he'd done it right by ordering her favorite foods and having them at the ready when she arrived. She never turned down mint chocolate pie from Sweet as Pie. "Sometimes I think you enjoy pushing my creative buttons."

"What gave you that idea?" Will lifted one corner of his mouth in that playful smile, but instead of thinking about all the single women in town who found it swoony, Janie felt a stirring of something in her belly. *A butterfly? Oh, no . . .*

"I need to sell more tickets to this charity event," she said, firmly set on changing the subject before she did something foolish like forget Will was her best friend and not this year's date for the holidays.

She reached for another ornament from the neatly packed box. Maybe Will didn't know much about decorating, but he *did* know a bit about handling the precious things. Every ornament was individually wrapped with tissue paper and care. "I've only sold two tickets since I took over. I've gone business to business, asking them for their support but that hasn't done much good. I even worked an extra shift at the restaurant so I could invite diners. Dad's lobster lasagna is what sold those two tickets."

"It's the best lobster lasagna in New England," Will said.

"Outside of standing on a street corner downtown and waving a sign—which I definitely don't have time to do—I'm out of ideas. If only I had more time to get the word out." She let out a sigh. "You have any bright ideas?"

"It's a dinner, you said?"

"Yep." She felt Grimm nudge her elbow before she could hang a clear candy cane ornament adorned in glitter. "You're right, buddy, it needs to go higher." She draped the ornament on an upper branch and rewarded the dog with fingers dug in behind his ears. She giggled at the sprinkles of red glitter on his nose.

The whole scene felt blissfully normal. Considering she usually spent the holidays running around with a date and barely made time to help Will wrap his gifts, she wasn't sure what to think about that. Will was familiar. There was no pressure to impress him. All benefits of a lifelong friendship. *Yes, familiar. That's all.*

"I'd guess people already have dinner plans on Christmas Eve," Will said. "Especially since this event isn't supposed to start until what? Seven?"

"Six thirty. You're probably right." The small town was filled mostly with families who gathered together on Christmas Eve. They prepared their own turkey dinners and went downtown as a unit for the tree lighting afterward, which didn't start until eight. "You'd think some people would like to get out of cooking."

"Not my family," Will said. "Grandma Annie wouldn't have it. She'd show up to the charity dinner and drag each and every Taggert back to her place by the ear." Only once when she was eleven had Janie had the opportunity to join in on one of Grandma Annie's famous Christmas Eve dinners. Will wasn't exaggerating. The meal was practically a production with gift opening after the generous dinner spread. More importantly, it was tradition.

"Maybe I should've let the town council cancel

—" A loud vibration cut her off. Grimm barked at the moving cell phone as it buzzed dangerously close to the edge of the coffee table. She scooped it up before it fell. "Hello?"

"Janie Arden?" an unfamiliar voice asked.

"Speaking. Who's this?"

"Sam Collins. You're the new event coordinator for the First Annual Snowy Falls Christmas Eve Charity Event, right?"

"Yes, I am." Janie remembered the name from the list of contacts the former event planner had left behind, but she couldn't place him immediately. She abandoned the tree for her tote bag on the couch, digging through it for her trusty planner. Grimm tried helping by wedging his nose inside the bag and licking her hand. "How can I help you"—Janie spotted his name on her list, next to *caterer*—"Mr. Collins?"

"I'm afraid I have some bad news."

Janie's stomach knotted and the brisk temperature in Will's house rose at least ten degrees. Maybe twenty. Whose bright idea had it been to wear a sweater? Oh right, hers. "Is there a menu change?" she asked, hopeful despite her gut warning her this was much worse than an unavailable ingredient.

"You might say that." Mr. Collins cackled on the other end, but it ended in a horrible cough.

"Mr. Collins, are you okay?"

"Afraid I've come down"—he coughed some

more—"with the flu. I doubt I'll be recovered in time."

"Can't anyone else fill in?"

"I'm a one-man operation, miss. There's no one else to call."

Janie felt Will's concern across the room, but she didn't dare look at him. Not yet. One glance would mean she didn't have this all handled. *No surrendering.* She could find a new caterer in time. No biggie. Christmas Eve was a whole three days away. "I'm sorry you're feeling under the weather, Mr. Collins. Please, feel better."

"Thank you for understanding."

"If you'll just let me know how you'll be refunding our deposit, I can let you get some much-needed rest." The silence on the other end made her stomach drop into her toes. "Mr. Collins?"

"It's a non-refundable deposit."

"But *we* didn't cancel you." She'd booked more than a few caterers for small events. All of them required a deposit. None of them refused to refund it if *they* backed out. It was a term she established before ever booking a caterer. But *she* hadn't booked Sam Collins.

"The money's been spent on ingredients." Sam sounded genuinely sorry, between his coughing fits.

Maybe if it weren't the holidays, Janie would press harder. She was representing the town of Snowy Falls, after all. But she couldn't stand the thought of putting a one-man business into the red because he got sick. She could be fierce when needed, but she wasn't Scrooge. "There's nothing left?"

"Twenty-three dollars."

Janie skimmed the notes left behind and nearly fell over at the amount already paid out to Sam Collins. *Forty-four hundred dollars.* It was Will's steadying hands on her shoulders that kept her knees from buckling. It was almost half her entire budget. Even if she could sell the rest of the tickets in time, she doubted she'd find a caterer who would work with little to no deposit. "That's it?"

"It was only the deposit. I don't bill for overhead costs until after the event, in case something like this happens. I can mail the check—"

"What's going to happen to all the ingredients you bought?"

"Already donated to the homeless shelter your fundraiser is for," Sam said, making her feel even worse for requesting the measly twenty-three dollars back. "I can't return any of it to the vendors, you see. I figured this was the next best thing. I've already spoken to the coordinator at the shelter, and she promises it'll all go to good use this Christmas."

Though Janie was surprised he hadn't consulted with her first to see if a replacement caterer could use the ingredients, she couldn't be upset about them being donated to people in need. She swallowed her frustration and simply said, "That was thoughtful of you, Mr. Collins."

"It was the least I could do." He coughed hard again. "I'm really sorry about this."

"Merry Christmas, Mr. Collins. I hope you feel better." Janie ended the call to ensure she wouldn't scream into the phone. The poor man may have been misguided in his judgment but he didn't deserve to be on the receiving end of her frustration. These circumstances were outside both their control.

A shaky hand dropped the phone onto the couch. She prided herself on being cool and collected during a crisis. But right now, she didn't feel anything remotely close to that. She felt like kicking and screaming and then ugly-crying as she ate the entire mint chocolate pie with one large spoon.

Will tugged her into his embrace, wrapping comforting arms around her like a warm blanket. Instantly, her rapidly beating heart slowed. "Deep breaths, Janie." Grimm pressed against the back of her legs with his massive body, pushing his head into her shoulder blade. The two of them made her feel instantly safe and secure. The Great Dane snuck a lick to her ear, eliciting a giggle.

"Thanks, Grimm." With surprising reluctance, Janie wriggled out of Will's embrace. Her arms tingled and her heart skipped a few beats, but she blamed it all on the overwhelming surge of panic brought on by a canceled caterer three days before the event.

"Want that chocolate pie now or after we finish the tree?" Will asked, the familiar kindness and compassion making her wish for things that could never be. They were too different. Too good of friends. Risking that lifelong bond of friendship over a moment of weakness was unnecessarily reckless.

"Let's finish the tree first. I need to feel like I've accomplished *something* today."

Will connected his phone to a speaker and played some upbeat holiday music. He always knew exactly how to bring her out of her funk, often before it had time to fully settle in. Had she been home when that call came in, she might've crawled into a corner and sobbed. Not something she'd ever admit to anyone, but reality just the same.

"What do you think I should do about the food?" Janie asked after the last of the ornaments were hung and they cleaned up loose tissue paper. "I don't know anyone who'd sign up to cater a big event last minute, especially right before the holidays. The stores are probably low on turkeys and all that anyway."

"Why not your—"

Janie's phone buzzed again, this time vibrating right off the edge of the coffee table. Grimm barked loudly at the device, growling low until Janie retrieved it. Another unknown number. "Great," she muttered before answering.

She felt Will watching her until the call ended, relieved she wasn't going through this alone. "The keynote speaker canceled too. Guess she won tickets to the Bahamas. Her flight leaves tomorrow morning." She dropped onto the couch, focusing on her breathing. Two or three more phone calls and there wouldn't be anything left to cancel.

"What kind of small-town charity dinner has a keynote speaker?" Will asked, joining her on the couch.

Janie shrugged in answer.

"Doesn't it seem odd to you?"

"I guess I never questioned it. She was going to speak about homelessness in New England. Raise awareness."

Grimm posted his front two paws in the gap between them and lifted high above them. His goofy face peered down at them both, as if pondering his next move. This wasn't the first time Janie encountered him trying not-so-subtly to be a lap dog.

"Grimm, buddy. We talked about this."

Ignoring Will's warning, Grimm crawled onto the couch, his every movement awkward as he settled into place. The couch was big, but not enough for all three of them to fit comfortably. Grimm grumbled as he looked back and forth and finally plopped down on the opposite side of Janie, pushing her against Will with sudden force.

"Grimm!" they said in unison.

Cheek pressed against Will's T-shirt, she couldn't help but inhale his woodsy cologne mixed with something Christmas-y. *Peppermint?* She glanced up, mesmerized by his lips. If he tilted his chin down, she could close the gap. *What's wrong with me?* "Grimm, this isn't funny," Janie grumbled.

"It's a little funny." Will peered down at her, that crooked smile drawing her attention back to his lips. She'd never thought about kissing her best friend before, so why was she thinking about it now?

"Okay, a little funny." Grimm's heavy body made it harder to breathe, but Janie was enjoying the excuse to be this close to Will more with each passing second. More than she should. Even if she ended up suffocated by the hundred-and-fifty-pound dog.

"You have some glitter." Will brushed his thumb against her cheek, the simple caress causing her entire body to erupt in delightful tingles. Her pulse quickened as once again her gaze landed on his lips. "Janie, I have—"

She groaned when her phone rang *again*. But it was less about who was canceling next and more about being interrupted. She should feel relieved that fate intercepted the *almost* kiss or they might've crossed a line in their friendship they couldn't uncross. So why was she so annoyed?

Will wrestled the dog off the couch, and Janie was somewhat sad he succeeded. Especially when the caller ID announced a spam call. *It's for the best. You don't go kissing your best friend, Janie. You know better.*

"What are you thinking, you big lug?" Will asked the dog, rubbing him along the neck. "You're bigger than the couch, buddy."

Janie dropped her phone into her tote bag, deciding anyone else who wanted to call this late could leave a voicemail or bother her tomorrow. If she had any sense, she'd leave Will to finish hanging the last few ornaments and head home. Maybe the only reason she was feeling something was because she'd been experiencing a vulnerable moment. Never mind that Will had been at her side through dozens—probably hundreds—of similar instances.

Instead of leaving, though, Janie turned and looked at Will. "You promised me mint chocolate pie."

"I did."

"And I bet Grimm is overdue for a treat."

The Great Dane plopped his bottom down so hard the couch shook.

"You've gone and done it now," Will teased as Janie hurried to the kitchen. Her favorite dessert might be the key to solving her most recent dilemma. She swore the pie had magic qualities. Surely a single bite would remind her she couldn't develop feelings for her best friend. Or maybe, it'd suggest just the opposite.

## CHAPTER 5

# WILL

"Grandma Annie!" Will lit up at the sight of the elderly woman marching into the fire station the next day with a stack of Christmas tins. Grimm awoke from his pre-lunch nap on his massive dog bed beside their smallest engine, instantly perking at the prospect of treats. "What are you doing here?"

"Baked too many snickerdoodles and thought you boys might be able to help me get rid of them." She refused any help offered and instead made a beeline right for the station breakroom, a trail of hungry firefighters following behind. Grimm trotted along with the rest, tail wagging in earnest.

"We can certainly help with that," Theron,

another firefighter, announced. He wasn't the only one eyeing the cookie tins on the round table. A lid popped off before Grandma Annie could unbutton her coat. From the wonderful cinnamon aroma the cookies sent into the air, Will suspected they were fresh out of the oven.

"Grandma Annie, you are too good to us." Will draped an arm over her shoulder in a side hug, watching as the chief snapped off a piece of his cookie and tossed it to Grimm. At least once a month, she *overbaked* and brought the extras to the station. December was his favorite month for her overachieving efforts.

She combed her fingers through her snow-white hair, taming the flyaways. "Gotta take care of our local heroes."

"Well, we certainly appreciate it, Mrs. Taggert," Chief Gundersen chimed in as the crew emptied one tin and opened a second.

"Make sure you save one for Phil," Grandma Annie instructed. "Heard he's out Christmas shopping with his wife today, but he'll never forgive me if I didn't leave him one."

"You got it," the chief confirmed.

Grimm trotted around the table and plopped at Grandma Annie's feet. Even sitting he came up to her shoulders. He leaned his head forward, welcoming soft pats. "You coming to reindeer bingo tonight?" she asked Will. "Jackpot's doubled since last Christmas. Two thousand smackaroos up for grabs."

"Didn't you win last year?"

"I did, just like I told Noah and Everly I would."

Will hadn't seen much of his eldest brother or his wife in the past couple of weeks. Mom mentioned something about Noah managing the health of the horses at Hartman Horse Farms so they could be cleared to give sleigh rides the week of Christmas. Every year it seemed the town added something new to their holiday festivities.

Maybe that's why Snowy Falls decided to throw a fancy Christmas Eve charity dinner better suited for a city. They were trying something new on for size, only even Will could tell it didn't fit right. The severe lack of ticket sales seemed to confirm his theory.

As if mere thoughts of his best friend summoned her, Janie burst into the breakroom. Though she smiled dutifully enough to fool everyone else, he saw through the façade with her usually styled hair all frizzy beneath the blue stocking hat. He'd bet his next paycheck she was frazzled about the event. They'd not only brainstormed possible solutions over mint chocolate pie last night until it was gone, but spent an hour on the phone after she got home as well.

Still, they were at a loss how to overcome all the challenges and sell those tickets.

Despite the setbacks, Will promised his best friend he wouldn't abandon her.

Time might be challenging to carve out with the family festivities, but he wasn't about to let her wrangle this massive event on her own. If Janie had planned the charity event from the beginning, she wouldn't need his help nearly as much. But she was inheriting someone else's mess. He wasn't going to stand idly by as one thing after another fell apart, even if her success meant she might leave for Boston without looking back.

"Janie, what a lovely surprise, dear." Grandma Annie pulled her in for a quick but tight hug. The petite woman often surprised people with her unexpectedly firm grip. "Did you stop by for my snicker-doodles?"

"I'm surprised half the town hasn't filed into the fire station by now," Janie said, grabbing one for herself. At the rate the firemen were going, there wouldn't be any left before long. "These are so good. Too bad you couldn't make some for the Christmas Eve charity event dinner. They'd draw a crowd for sure."

"Have you bought a ticket yet?" Will asked Grandma Annie as the guys cleared out of the break-room, leaving behind mere crumbs in the tins. He already knew the answer, but he hoped asking might prompt some help, or at least words of wisdom.

Grandma Annie knew everyone in Snowy Falls, and everyone knew her.

"Nope. Not buying one either." Grandma Annie tossed away the wax paper liners and closed the lids on the empty tins. "Not my cup of tea. The whole thing's too fancy. Not just for my tastes. For a small town. Plus, the timing's all wrong. Move it to earlier in the day, throw in some reindeer bingo and Christmas caroling, and *then* I might reconsider."

"At this rate, we might have to," Will mumbled.

Grandma Annie patted him on the shoulder. "I need to get the rest of my Christmas shopping done before Blakely comes over." Will's youngest sister was unanimously voted to be Grandma Annie's personal assistant in the kitchen this holiday season, mostly to ensure she wouldn't run off and try to elope again. "You'll see to it that I get that last tin back?" she asked Will, nodding at the only container with cookies left in it.

"Of course."

Will felt a tug on his sleeve as Grandma Annie hustled down the hallway and disappeared into the bay.

"Will, that's it!" Janie said.

"What is?"

"The event. It's too fancy. It's too much flashy city gala and not enough small-town fun." She turned in a full circle until she spotted a notepad on a side counter. She grabbed it and a pencil and dropped into a worn chair, yanking him down in the seat beside her.

"I don't understand," Will admitted, helping himself to one of the last cookies though he ended up sharing half of it with Grimm.

"We've been looking at this all wrong," Janie insisted, scribbling notes so quickly it was a wonder to watch her hand move. "The whole charity dinner —it's all wrong. It might work in a place like Boston or New York City, but not Snowy Falls. I have to start over. From scratch."

"Janie, Christmas Eve is only two days away."

"I know." When she looked up at him, her expression was void of any anxiety from earlier. Excitement twinkled in her eyes. The way they illuminated made her even more attractive. "It's crazy, right? I know it's crazy. But it's either I redesign the whole thing or the event ends up canceled anyway." She hastily jotted one list item after another. "Grandma Annie's right. We need games and holiday music. But that's just for starters. This event needs to speak to families, not just adults. Oh, did I mention our decorating service canceled too?" She laughed, not a trace of panic or gloom in her expression as there had been last night. "Apparently their truck was T-boned by someone running a red light and all their decorations spilled out in the intersection. Figures, huh?"

Watching passion ignite in Janie was a wonder

all its own. It was the reason Will so easily fell in love with her in the sixth grade. Back then, it was over a science project. She wasn't satisfied with making a regular exploding volcano. She wanted to go all out, and her excitement was all it took to convince Will as her lab partner to take the risk. In the end, they earned a B for straying from the instructions. But Mrs. Nelson *had* been impressed.

"We might have to rally some local troops to donate Christmas decorations. I don't know if you saw that auditorium, but yikes. It looks like a place Scrooge would hang out to avoid the holidays. Do they still do phone trees in this town? I don't know how many people would check social media in time."

"You don't need a phone tree."

"No?"

The Taggert attic was filled to the brim with Christmas decorations. Too many to ever unpack and use all in one holiday on three houses, let alone one. Even on a house as massive as the one Will grew up in. "You've never seen my parents' attic, have you?"

"No," Janie said. "We stole the key and tried to sneak up there once, but your dad caught us before I could even poke my head up there. You always made it sound like this magical place, though."

Will laughed in memory. "Well, at that age, we were a little—"

"Accident prone?"

"You wouldn't believe how many breakable items are up there." Will was only ever granted access to the attic growing up when he was tasked with hauling things up or down for Christmas. "But we're older now. I'm sure she'd make an exception for you."

"Me?" Janie gaped playfully. "I'm not the one who broke my arm when I fell off the roof."

"I only fell because you tripped and threw me off balance."

Janie rolled her eyes in a manner he could only describe as flirtatious. It was more than wishful thinking, of that he felt certain. Maybe he'd get that Christmas wish after all. "I'm not that girl anymore, Will."

Maybe she'd outgrown her clumsy phase, but he would forever notice every little way she *was* still the girl he'd grown up with and came to love. They'd been inseparable their entire childhood. He knew in his heart they were destined to be together someday. Except, Janie started dating other boys and never once considered him as anything more than a friend.

*Time to change that.*

"I have so much to coordinate. Do you think the chief would let you run around and help me if I bribed him with free dinner at The Twisted Lobster through Christmas?" Janie asked with a laugh, her tone implying the idea was only *partially* a joke.

Will hated to ask for the time away only because he'd heard yet another rumor that Oscar Freeman would be retired before summer. As things stood now, Will felt he was a surefire candidate for the deputy fire chief position once it opened. But he wasn't without competition. "I'm off tomorrow," Will offered. "Can't you work from the breakroom a little longer?"

"I have to make new flyers right away and get them up all over town. It can't wait." Janie was out of her seat before he had time to ask her where she was headed. "Everyone needs to know we're moving up the time of the event and adding family-friendly activities."

He and Grimm were left to rush after her. They weren't quick enough to stop Janie from approaching Chief Gundersen.

"Will would never ask you himself because of his strong sense of duty to his community," Janie said. "But the First Annual Snowy Falls Christmas Eve Charity Event is *also* important to Snowy Falls. It would be a good thing for the local fire department to have a representative, don't you think?"

"I suppose it wouldn't hurt," the chief mused.

"I've performed some event planning miracles," Janie added before the chief could say more. "But with only two short days before the event, I'm not sure I can pull it off without Will's help. I'd be more than happy to repay the favor when the time comes."

Will's pulse quickened, afraid to hope for more time with Janie. Maybe that Christmas magic

Grandma Annie was always going on about was not only real, but more importantly, on his side this year.

"You'll help plan our annual pancake breakfast?" Chief Gundersen asked.

Janie shook his hand. "Consider it done."

## CHAPTER 6

# JANIE

It didn't matter how many times Janie ordered her dad's famous lobster mac and cheese, it would always be her absolute favorite dish. She quietly moaned in delight at the first bite of food she'd had all day. With all the running around posting flyers on every light post and storefront window, she'd forgotten all about eating.

If it weren't for Will insisting they stop for an early dinner at The Twisted Lobster before they tackled Robyn's attic for Christmas decorations, she might've kept going all day on an empty stomach. But her best friend knew all too well how cranky she got once she hit *that* point. It was better for both of them if she was fed.

She looked up at Will, watching him cut into his lobster lasagna, wondering if she'd ever truly appreciated how much he was there for her whenever she needed him. Nearly everyone who'd been lined up to help with the original event had canceled. Only the representative from the toy drive and the dessert order from Sweet as Pie were a go. Every other aspect of the event was brand new.

Will was not only by her side through all the ups and downs these past couple of days, but enthusiastic about it all. Best yet, he believed in her. When her traitorous gaze dropped to his lips, she quickly looked away. Thinking about that kiss that almost was but ultimately wasn't wouldn't do her any favors.

"I'm so glad you convinced your parents to cater the event," Will said as he polished off the last bite and sat back in his chair.

"I know it's not a traditional Christmas dinner," admitted Janie.

"That's the best part. Now we don't have to figure out how to cook a couple dozen turkeys."

They'd revised the timing of the event, moving it to early afternoon at Grandma Annie's suggestion and ending two hours before the parade preceding the Christmas Eve tree lighting ceremony began. Now residents wouldn't be expected to pick attending the charity dinner over their own family gatherings. They could manage both and still make it to the most traditional town events in the evening.

Janie wondered if the previous event planner had ever visited Snowy Falls. It seemed glaringly obvious she didn't understand the town, which oddly enough, brought out Janie's protective instincts. In the future after Janie relocated to Boston, would the city council hire outsider event planners who'd make the same mistake?

"Do you even know *how* to cook a turkey?" Janie asked Will.

"Sure, I do. Dad taught me. But that doesn't mean I have the longing to make one. Or thirty." Will emptied his soda. "I think using a local restaurant instead of some one-man show out of Boston was a better decision anyway. And great exposure for a local business."

"I agree." Secretly, Janie hoped it would be the solution to two problems. Yes, it meant extra hours for her parents to prep everything last minute. But hopefully it would drum up enough future business to keep the restaurant firmly in the black. If she still left for Boston, she wanted to be sure they'd be okay. *If?* Janie felt an odd flutter in her stomach, uncertain if it was butterflies or dread. If *I go to Boston?*

"You okay?" Will asked. "You look like you swallowed a lemon or something."

"Or something."

"Janie?"

"It's nothing." She pushed aside her empty bowl to make room for her planner, and opened it. "Did I tell you I have a new photographer lined up?" Janie ran a finger down her bullet-pointed list, ignoring Will's assessing gaze. "Thankfully the one who canceled wasn't given a deposit to begin with."

"That's great news."

"Well, she's a pet photographer. But beggars can't be choosers and all that. Figured if she can get dogs and cats to cooperate, she can handle kids." Janie made a note to set up a photo booth in the corner nearest Santa, hopeful the photographer could juggle both the quirky booth photos and kids sitting in Santa's lap. They were lucky enough to secure one photographer. Two was out of the question.

"How's that list coming?" Mom asked, clearing away their empty bowls. A pang of guilt hit Janie, reminding her that instead of sitting at a table, she should be the one clearing away the plates. Her parents were shorthanded as it was, but Janie hadn't taken that into consideration when she volunteered to take over this event. The shifts she normally worked had been forfeited, the extra work falling to her parents and a couple other servers.

"Getting there," Janie answered. "Do you want me to wash some dishes or something while I'm here? I could do a grocery run—"

Mom silenced her with a firm glare, the look all

the answer she needed. She loved how much her parents supported her, even when she took on insane tasks that ate up entire shifts. "We've got things handled, Janie. You can wash all the dishes you want after Christmas." With a wink, Mom returned to the kitchen.

"Do we have everything set up for the toy drive?" Will asked.

"I need to line up a couple more gift wrappers, but otherwise that's a go." Janie skimmed the list, feeling both accomplished and stir-crazy. In half a day, she'd managed to give the charity event a whole new face. One that promised family entertainment as opposed to a stuffy, formal dinner. Local businesses gladly donated door prizes and auction items. Over two dozen people had volunteered to work during the event. Tickets were selling at a steady rate. Best of all, Grandma Annie was making extra batches of snickerdoodle cookies.

She felt a sense of pride for what she'd pulled off in record time, even if this family-friendly event was in direct contradiction with the types of formal events she desired to create. She could have easily stayed with the elegant, too-fancy theme and done a spectacular job for the few patrons who attended. But instinctually, she knew it was all wrong for Snowy Falls.

"I would ask my sisters to help with gift wrapping, but they're all tied up this year. Blakely would gladly volunteer, if only to get out of helping Grandma Annie in the kitchen. But then you'd have to deal with the wrath—"

"No, thanks!" Janie interrupted with a laugh. "I don't have a death wish, you know." She closed her planner and scooted out of her seat. "I need to make a call about tablecloths and stop by the floral shop to see about poinsettias." Janie shrugged into her coat. "Are you coming?"

"I need to pick up Grimm from the fire station. Can we stop there first?"

Though Janie's parents loved Grimm, the health inspector wasn't crazy about finding dog hair inside the restaurant. At least this coming summer he could sit outside with Will on the patio. She pictured the duo eating lobster lasagna on the patio without her, possibly with one of the many single women who practically swooned at the sight of Will, and frowned.

## CHAPTER 7

ILL

Grimm whined excitedly as Will pulled up alongside his parents' two-story brick house. His buddy Tango waited at the window, tongue hanging out the side of his mouth. Though the family dog was nearing a decade in age, the lab was always up for tug-of-war with Grimm. "Hold on, buddy. We'll be inside in a minute."

Christmas lights twinkled through the living room window. He suspected Mom had the fattest tree with the most strands of lights in all of Snowy Falls this year. She certainly had enough ornaments to cover ten. Her theme changed each holiday season, which was why the attic was filled with enough decorations to deck out the city hall auditorium twice over.

"Is it weird that I feel giddy?" Janie asked, wearing a crooked smile. It drew his attention to her lips, as it often did. Only this time, it reminded him of the missed opportunity last night. If that spam call hadn't interrupted them, where would they be now? Would one kiss have changed everything between them for the better? *Or for the worse?*

"You've been granted rare permission to enter Mom's alternate reality. It's a special day." He dared to hook a loose curl caught in her stocking hat with his finger and pull it free from its snare on the fabric, noticing the way Janie's eyes darkened a single shade at his proximity. With any luck, future moments like this would conclude with a kiss. For now, he settled for gently dragging a finger down her cheek before he dropped his hand. "Seeing the attic for the first time is an experience I don't think you can ever fully prepare for."

Her cheeks reddened, but whether from his touch or the sudden rush of cold air when she pushed open the door, he wasn't certain. "I *do* feel like I've won a golden ticket," Janie admitted as Will secured Grimm's leash. Chances were he'd bolt straight for the front door to greet his friend. But a squirrel could unravel best laid plans.

Tango, a blond lab-husky mix, nudged aside the curtain as he reappeared in the window, his nose getting stuck in the sheer fabric this time. Grimm whined. "He's just tangled with excitement to see you," Will said with a laugh. "You can rescue him soon enough."

"I can't believe how well Grimm gets along with nearly everyone and every creature," Janie said. "Even cats like him."

"He is pretty great, huh?" Will smiled in memory of Grimm's ridiculous attempt to be a lap dog pushing Janie closer to him last night on the couch. How close he'd come to finally kissing her after all these years of wondering what it'd be like. All because the Great Dane wanted to be part of the pack. Yeah, Grimm was pretty perfect.

"Oh good, you're here," Mom said as she opened the door to them, greeting them both with a warm smile and an even warmer hug. "I made caramel corn. It's almost cool enough to eat. I'll have you try some if you don't mind being guinea pigs."

"This holiday season's turning out be quite dangerous for my waistline," Janie said with a laugh. "Good thing I hardly have a minute to sit down until it's over."

Automatically, Will's gaze swept over Janie's petite, slightly curvy figure. She was perfect in every way. No amount of caramel corn or snickerdoodles would have the least effect on how he saw her. She'd always be the most beautiful woman in any room.

Grimm charged into the house, darting for Tango

who held a red and green rope toy with his teeth. One Chloe made for him last Christmas. "Come on inside, you two. Your father'll have a fit if you let out all the heat, you know." Mom waved them in, quickly closing the door behind them. "No need to wake him from his late afternoon nap before we need to load up the trailer."

Will and Janie shed coats, gloves, and snow-covered boots at the door as the dogs ran circles around the main floor. "He sleeps through that?" Janie asked, pointing at the dogs.

"He's out like a light unless he feels a cold draft," Will answered, sharing a quick smile with Janie that warmed him from the inside out.

She looked away first. "I really appreciate you sharing your Christmas decorations with us," Janie said to Mom. "I have no idea what the last event planner had in mind since she left zero notes on that subject. Her décor service wasn't much help on the phone or via their website, which was down. I'm working with a blank canvas."

"I have more than enough to decorate that town hall twice over." Mom handed Janie a pair of slippers and waved for them to follow her up the hardwood staircase. Will resisted the urge to grab the banister since it was wrapped in greenery with pinecones and red ornaments that matched the runner rug.

"Twice over?" He understood the doubt in

Janie's eyes considering the entire Taggert house was decorated thoroughly for the holidays.

"At least," Mom said, not missing a beat. "Every year that auditorium is cold and completely lacking in holiday spirit. It should be a crime when a few donations would spruce the place right up. Wouldn't require a dime out of the city's budget, you know."

"With any luck, this charity event will be the first of many," Janie added as Mom led them down the hall where he and his brothers had slept as kids. He'd bunked with Cole for a number of years, but their old room had been converted into Mom's craft room. He wondered if Janie remembered the *no girls allowed* sign that used to hang from the door. The same one they ignored on multiple occasions, much to Cole's consternation.

He wanted so badly to believe their connection was deeper than friendship. He felt certain he was no longer imagining the sparks between them. The stolen glances and secret smiles that flirted with a deeper connection. But one misstep and he could ruin a decade plus-long friendship.

At the attic door, Mom pulled a key out of her pocket. "You're welcome to any of the wreaths up there. Christmas trees, lights, and ornaments too. I have a few sentimental items I don't want to offer up so they don't get lost or broken. But most of the decorations are fair game."

"You *still* keep this door locked?" Janie asked as

Mom inserted the key into the lock and twisted, voicing the surprise he felt considering none of his siblings lived at home anymore.

"I keep all the presents up there," Mom said conspiratorially to Janie. "Ben has always been the worst at sneaking peeks. Twice as bad as any of the kids ever were." A cool draft breezed past them as Mom opened the door and nodded for them to follow her. "But don't worry. I have them locked in a closet, and you don't have that key."

The stairs creaked at their weight, the familiar aroma of cinnamon pinecones overwhelming them with each step. If Will lived to be a hundred, this was the scent he'd remember for the rest of his life. The smell of family Christmas.

"Oh, my goodness." At the top of the stairs, Janie's eyes grew to twice their usual size as she scanned the attic. The staircase split the expansive space into two sections. The walkways were the only clear areas. Every other inch, including the walls and rafters, was adorned with Christmas decorations.

"Christmas trees, wreaths, garland, and basically any greenery are on the south side," Mom informed them with a wave of her hand. "Ornaments, snow-men, and Santas are on the north end. Totes are in the east corner. Fill as many as you need. I'll get Ben to help us load. We have a covered trailer, and I think it'll get most of the decorations moved in one trip."

Janie moved her lips, as if she were trying to

speak but couldn't quite form words. The first time Will had been allowed in the attic, he remembered the same speechlessness come over him.

"Thanks, Mom. We'll get to work."

"I'll grab you kids some caramel corn and hot cocoa before I wake your father."

"This is unbelievable," Janie said, eyes wide as she slowly stepped into the greenery overload on the south side. Even with everything Mom had already used to decorate the house, there was still only narrow aisles of walking space. With each step, tree branches caught on their elbows. "I have no words."

"You haven't even seen how many decorations she used in the house yet." Will followed her as she wandered through the artificial tree forest. Or at least that's what he'd always called it. All it was missing was a blanket of fresh snow.

"Your mom doesn't use real trees?" Janie asked.

"Mom switched to fake trees years ago because the family dog—Zoey at the time—had a tendency to drink the real ones dry."

Janie turned back to look at him. "I remember Zoey. She was a sweetheart."

"And a rambunctious ball of energy."

"Has your family ever *not* had a dog?" Janie asked as she wove through the edge of the artificial trees and turned down an aisle of Christmas wreaths. Dozens of homemade creations hung from a lattice wall, each one unique.

"No, I don't think so. Mom and Dad met because of a dog."

"I didn't know that."

Will reached for a wreath sprayed with fake snow, wondering why Mom never set up a booth at a craft show. She'd make a killing selling her homemade wreaths. Each one was made with such care and had such exquisite detail. "Yeah, Dad's dog got loose and ran after a squirrel. Hurried past Mom and startled her so badly she fell backward into a snowbank. When Dad stopped to help her up, the dog stopped chasing the squirrel. Almost as if—"

"The dog was playing matchmaker?" Janie asked, stopping in the middle of the Christmas wreath display to look at him. In such confined quarters, it was difficult *not* to be sandwiched together. He wondered if she could hear the pounding of his heart.

"Yeah, something like that." Dogs had a habit of bringing his family together with the ones they were meant to be with. It'd happened to both Noah and Chloe last Christmas. He wondered if Grimm had any tricks up his sleeve to ensure it happened for Will *this* holiday season.

When the lattice wall ended, Will spotted a stack of empty totes in the corner. But before he could figure out a path to them, he nearly collided into Janie. "What are—" He followed her gaze up to the rafter above them. It wasn't simply one bundle of mistletoe tied together with a red ribbon. It was *dozens*.

Janie shuffled forward pretending not to notice what dangled above them. Will stayed close behind wishing he could use this opportunity to test the waters but not wanting to spook her any more than she obviously already was. Until they reached a dead-end. Boxed in by stacked totes and giant snowmen and Santa decorations, there was no way out of mistletoe row without retreating the way they'd come.

Janie turned suddenly, nearly bumping into his chest as she kept stealing quick glances overhead. "Can we, um—"

"Are you okay?" Will asked, confused by the shininess in her eyes. He recognized the panic, but didn't understand why she felt it now. Was it *him*? Would tugging her into his embrace calm her as it had other times, or make the whole situation worse?

"Yeah. I'm just—"

"What?"

She cleared her throat and pasted a smile across her lips that he saw right through. "This would be perfect for a Christmas kissing photo booth, don't you think?" She reached up toward the longest piece and let her fingers gently comb through it. "Almost comical, right? You can dodge one piece of hanging mistletoe, but a hundred?"

"You really think there's a hundred?" he asked,

relieved to feel the tension between them dissipate. The twinkling light in her eyes reassured him of it.

"At least. Maybe more."

"Does that mean you're supposed to kiss someone a hundred times?" He curled one side of his mouth in a mischievous smile, relieved when she laughed at his question when she could have so easily shut down instead.

"Wouldn't your lips get tired?" she teased.

"Depends on who you're kissing, I suppose." Will risked hooking a loose blonde curl and tucking it behind her ear, his fingertips tingling as they caressed her soft cheek. "Either way, you realize it'd be bad luck *not* to kiss you at least once right now, right?"

"The last thing I need is bad luck." Janie bit down on her bottom lip as he cupped her jaw and tilted her chin up. Every movement remained cautious yet deliberate. Their gazes locked as he leaned down to meet her parted lips. Thrill and terror warred inside him as her gaze dropped to his lips. One kiss could change everything. One kiss *would* change everything. But *how* was the only question that mattered, and the only one he had no definitive answers for. He risked it all and lowered his lips the rest of the way.

Gently, he brushed a kiss onto Janie's eager lips and felt his world forever change. His pulse raced as she melted against him, her palm flattening against his chest as the kiss deepened. He felt dizzy, as if the attic were spinning around them. Time seemed to stand still for this very important moment that awakened his soul.

"I ran out of candy canes," Mom announced as the creaking stairs echoed. "I'm afraid you'll have to drink your cocoa without since someone raided my stash."

Will and Janie hopped apart, alarm dancing in Janie's eyes but a giddy smile on her freshly kissed lips. They scurried back the way they came, both grabbing armfuls of wreaths on their way in an unspoken, shared conspiracy to keep their adventures in mistletoe row a secret.

"Coming, Mom."

# JANIE

It was close to midnight, yet nearly two dozen volunteers worked tirelessly into the night. Half the fire department worked to unload the Taggert trailer at the city hall while other volunteers sorted piles of decorations throughout the auditorium. Janie took inventory of wreaths, garlands, and Christmas lights as a vision for the overall design played in her head. It was her favorite part of event planning—the creative portion that didn't require a checklist or list of instructions. Her imagination called the shots and magic brought it all to life.

"It's really coming together." Chloe offered Janie

a cup of coffee. It wasn't her preferred white chocolate mocha from The Maine Bean, but it was refreshing just the same. The very nectar that would give her another hour of steam before she had nothing left but fumes. At least there was one full day to go before the event.

"All thanks to your mom's generosity."

"You mean her talent for hoarding Christmas in the attic?" Chloe teased.

Janie blushed at the very mention of the place where Will had cupped her cheek and drew her in for a kiss that *still* curled her toes to think about. She wasn't supposed to feel that way about kissing her best friend. She wasn't supposed to *kiss* her best friend. Yet, she wondered if she'd subconsciously marched right into mistletoe row knowing she could blame the Christmas tradition for the very kiss she'd been craving since Grimm decided to play lap dog the other night at Will's.

"Everything okay?" Chloe asked, helping Janie untangle the strand of snowflake lights she planned to use for the photo booth.

"Just tired." Careful to avoid direct eye contact with Will's oldest sister, Janie counted three strands of snowflake lights, hoping it'd be enough.

"Well, you have been running nonstop since you volunteered to take this over. Or so my brother says."

"Yes." Janie had to admit she hadn't worked this hard to pull together a last-minute event in a long time. She felt more exhilarated to see it all come together than tired from the effort involved. But it was easier to let Chloe think she was worn out than admit she was plotting how to steal another mistletoe-induced kiss. "I hope Snowy Falls loves all the changes. It's nothing like the original event."

"That's what makes it so perfect. *You* actually know and understand the town. That last event planner obviously did not." Chloe opened another tote and unloaded the contents on the table for Janie to inventory. "There're a few locals who would've loved a chance to get all dressed up, but fewer still who would've abandoned their own Christmas Eve dinners for this one."

"I had plenty of offers for donations before, but not ticket sales." With the event revised, they'd run out of tickets earlier today and had to have more printed. It was a nice problem to have, especially since there wasn't reserved seating limiting the turnout. "I really have Grandma Annie to thank. It was her comment that gave me the epiphany."

"She always seems to know what to say, doesn't she?"

Janie flirted with the idea of asking Grandma Annie for advice about Will, but dismissed it before she had time to take it seriously. It didn't stop her gaze from landing on her best friend across the room, carrying in Christmas trees, however.

"It's a shame Will doesn't have a date for

Grandma Annie's Christmas Eve feast this year," Chloe said, her tone nonchalant though her eyes twinkled with familiar mischief. Janie wasn't close with Will's sisters, but she knew them well enough to know Chloe was the most perceptive when it came to these things. Likely that trait helped her find the perfect home for each unique dog she rescued.

"You know Will. All he needs is—"

"Grimm."

The two women looked at each other and laughed.

"You don't think there's a reason he hasn't dated all this time, do you?"

"He's picky, for one," Janie said as she sorted through a variety of red and gold garland. "Says he knows what he's looking for and doesn't waste his time—or anyone else's—if he already knows from the start it won't work." Which only made the kiss all the more confusing. They'd been under dozens of mistletoe arrangements, and it *was* bad luck not to kiss someone in that situation. But would Will have kissed anyone else beneath it or found an excuse to escape with a peck on the cheek? Hadn't Janie seen him do just that last Christmas when he was trapped under the mistletoe with Jillie Marsh at the fire station's holiday party? "Will claims he has a sense of people, kind of like Grimm."

"Grimm loves everyone. Except anyone Blakely dates or tries to marry." Chloe let out a laugh. "But sounds like something my stubborn brother would say. Won't even entertain a date because he's convinced it's doomed before it starts."

"I tried to talk him into asking out Alicia Meadows. You know, the third-grade teacher. But obviously he didn't take my advice." With the earlier kiss still buzzing across her lips she felt oddly relieved he ignored her insistence that he ask the beautiful young teacher to be his date for the Christmas Eve charity event.

"What about you?" Chloe asked.

Janie felt the heat creep up her neck instantly and ducked her head toward the clipboard, hopeful her frizzy blonde hair would hide the blush. "Me?" She nearly choked on the word.

"You *always* have a date for the holidays," Chloe added. "Not this year?"

The relief washed over her, like a much-needed cool breeze on a stiflingly hot day. "I decided this year I was going to focus on getting my event planning business officially off the ground. A boyfriend would've distracted me and put it off another year. It was time to break the pattern."

"But you already *do* have your own business," Chloe countered. "At least that's what half of Snowy Falls would say if you asked them for an event planner referral."

Janie doubted that, especially since she'd volunteered her services at the council meeting rather than been recommended by anyone in the audience. "I plan small events on the side, around shifts at The Twisted Lobster," she admitted. "But I want to do this full time. I want an official office where I can meet with clients to discuss bigger and fancier events. Galas, charity auction dinners, awards banquets. That sort of thing." But that familiar zing of excitement didn't rush through her quite as enthusiastically as it usually did.

"*This* is a big event," Chloe said.

"In a small town." She mumbled the last under her breath, her gaze again landing on Will. This time he caught her staring and sent her a smile back. Her heart pitter-pattered in an odd flutter. She blamed mistletoe row and the complication it added to their friendship. *You want it to be more than that and you know it, Janie.*

"What about you and Will?" Chloe asked, her question not only aptly timed but unapologetically blunt. "I hope you don't mind my saying so, but I always thought you two would make such a cute couple."

"We're just friends."

Chloe rolled her eyes. "So I keep hearing."

"I've never let myself go there, you know? I don't want to ruin what we have. We've been friends since the sixth grade." She tried to say that Will was like a brother to her, but the lie tangled on her tongue and never made it past her lips.

"It's a risk," Chloe agreed, lifting the empty tote. "One only you can decide if it's worth taking."

Janie watched her carry the tote to the opposite end of the auditorium, more confused than ever. It was no longer possible but probable that Janie was falling for her best friend. Despite the earlier kiss, however, they could still comfortably remain friends. They were tiptoeing the line that, if crossed, could never be uncrossed. It would be so much easier to step back into their comfort zone and stay there. *But it's not what you want.*

Feeling overwhelmed and a bit overheated, Janie slipped away from her table and down a deserted hallway.

She leaned against the cold brick, closing her eyes as she allowed her head to fall back against the wall. With a couple of deep breaths, Janie pictured herself in Boston at Christmas, strolling down the city sidewalk in her fanciest dress to one of Erin Carlile's elite events. The bustling city with decorated light posts and storefronts. The chatter of excited patrons entering the gala through grand double doors. It was the same picture she'd imagined for years. Except this time when she envisioned a date on her arm, it was Will.

Would it be so crazy to ask him to move to Boston *with* her when the time came? As a firefighter, he could easily find a job. The city offered several dog parks for Grimm. They would only be an hour or two away. Close enough to still visit family and friends in Snowy Falls. Janie had only to take a chance, as Chloe said.

A wet smear across her hand startled a squeak from Janie as her eyes popped open. "Grimm, you scared me." The Great Dane licked her hand until she moved her fingers to his favorite spot right behind his ears. She searched the hall for Will, but it was only the two of them. She rested her cheek against the top of Grimm's head. "How did you know I was out here, buddy?"

Grimm wagged his tail in response.

"I wish you could talk. Maybe *you* could tell me what to do." She let out a sigh that turned into a yawn, reminding her how late it was. They still had an entire day to decorate the auditorium and set up all the stations and tables. As long as everything was unloaded, she should send the volunteers home for the night.

Janie made it halfway down the hall before she heard voices. The double doors leading into the main room were propped open, and she stopped short of them. Grimm stopped with her, tilting his head at her with that adorably excited expression and perked ears that seemed to question if they were on a secret spy mission together.

"You didn't hear this from me," a deep voice said. One that sounded an awful lot like Fire Chief Gundersen. "But Oscar requested to retire sooner than planned. He's been eligible for the past two years and his wife's been on him, so I can't say I'm surprised."

"I heard the spring." *Will.* That was definitely Will's voice.

"Mid-January."

"That soon?" Will asked, sounding as shocked as Janie felt.

"You have everything in order?" the chief asked, his tone lowering even more. Janie had to creep closer to hear better, but Grimm's click-clacking claws threatened to give away their position.

"I have a few Ts to cross yet," Will admitted.

"Get on that sooner rather than later," the chief said. "Unless you've changed your mind about the position?"

"No, sir. I want it. Snowy Falls is my home. Always has been." Janie felt a pang of disappointment at his answer, even though it was expected. Will had told her a few times how the chief had hinted he was a shoe-in for the deputy fire chief position when it opened. He had competition, but Will was the unspoken favorite. A man born and raised in Snowy Falls who loved his hometown with all his heart.

Grimm whined. "Shh!" Janie shushed the dog, but it was too late. The halted conversation warned her she needed to come out of hiding or duck through the nearest door before someone caught her.

Abandoned by her four-legged spy partner, Janie fell into a janitor's closet.

"Grimm, where did you come from?" Will's voice echoed down the hall, but Janie didn't dare open the door. She needed a moment to compose herself before she sent the volunteers home. Earlier fantasy shattered, she realized she could no more ask Will to move to Boston and give up the fire station and hometown he loved than she could give up her own dream in order to stay.

They'd have to remain friends who once shared a kiss under the mistletoe. Maybe one day when they'd both chased their dreams, they could even laugh about it. But the thought left a sour expression on Janie's face and a twist in her stomach.

## CHAPTER 9

ILL

"You're playing Santa?" Ms. Meadows asked in the holiday party aisle of Snowy Falls Gifts and Treasures, her kind eyes twinkling with interest. Interest he could never entertain, much less return. Not after that life-altering kiss he'd shared with Janie beneath that mistletoe-clad rafter yesterday. That kiss told him everything he needed to know.

"I am," Will said, still laying on the charm for the sake of the event. "But don't tell your third graders that."

She reached out and touched his arm playfully. "But I can tell them Grimm's playing Santa's helper, right?"

Discreetly and without losing his smile, Will shrugged his arm free of her fingers. "Absolutely. Grimm would love to see them and show off his red candy cane bandana." The only reason he was in his fourth local gift shop in thirty minutes was because he promised Janie he'd find the last of the holiday-themed napkins in town. She'd shoved a couple dozen tickets in his coat pocket before he left the auditorium, hopeful he could sell them before his return. "Can we count on you to attend?"

Ms. Meadows reached into her purse, retrieving cash. "I wouldn't miss it, *Santa*."

"Great, see you there." Tucking the money into his pocket, Will dashed around the corner to avoid any uncomfortable topics of conversation that might follow. Ms. Meadows wasn't the only single woman in Snowy Falls who shamelessly flirted with him in hopes for more. But maybe this Christmas, he could finally stop all the unwanted attention with a girlfriend on his arm—Janie Arden.

After that kiss, Will felt more confident than ever that they were meant to be. He'd dreamed of that moment for years, and yet it still hadn't prepared him for the way the world disappeared around them when their lips met.

"Excuse me. Do you know if this store has any of those homemade peanut butter dog treats?" a woman asked Will, instantly setting off his instinct to flee. But he relaxed the moment her large, shiny diamond caught the light and nearly blinded him. "Chloe's K-9 Creations," the woman added. "That's the brand. I haven't been able to find them in any of the usual stores. Seems everyone is sold out. I heard they're made right here in Snowy Falls, though."

"They're usually at the front counter," Will said, pointing.

The woman seemed too elegant for a small town. Her hair perfectly styled, her makeup expertly applied, her outfit expensive. Even her red manicured nails seemed pricey. "I already checked there." She let out a sigh, disappointment etched into her expression. He'd have to tell Chloe how popular her treats had become. "Do you know anywhere else in town that's selling them? I've been to four stores already, and they're all sold out. My daughter's beside herself. She's convinced every other dog treat out there isn't good enough for our Chowder. Especially not for Christmas."

"You've traveled a long way?"

"From Boston."

Will studied the woman a little closer, wondering if he'd seen her before or why it felt as if he had. Surely, he'd remember someone so refined in quaint Snowy Falls.

"Erin?" a man called to her as he approached. He draped an arm over her shoulder and started to steer her away with his hand. "They're sold out here too. I don't think we're going to find any this year.

We need to get back or we'll be late to the event tonight."

"Erin," Will repeated, not meaning to speak the name aloud but it slipping out anyway. It turned their heads, stopping them from walking away. It suddenly struck Will why he recognized the poised woman. "You wouldn't by chance be Erin *Carlile?*"

"I am." The recognition seemed to give her eyes a dim illumination. "Do I know you?"

"Not exactly." Will's pulse quickened as he realized the dilemma before him. This woman was Janie's event planner idol. Janie needed those napkins, but she'd never forgive him if he didn't try to help Erin. "Chloe's my sister."

"Really?"

"Let me give her a quick call." He fished his phone from his pocket, his stack of tickets spilling out onto the floor as he did. He crouched to collect them as the phone rang, wondering if this was more than simply a coincidental meeting. He knew what Grandma Annie would say about such things. She didn't believe in coincidences. Add in the time of year, and she'd explain it with Christmas magic.

"Will, what's up?" Chloe asked, reminding him he was on the phone.

"Hey, do you have any of your famous peanut butter dog biscuits left? There's a couple in town who've traveled all the way from Boston to find some."

"I'm sorry. I'm all out. I planned to make more, but George turned out to be a bigger handful than I expected. He ate my last batch. The *whole* thing. Needless to say, he's in timeout right now."

Will breathed a sigh, but whether of relief or disappointment, he wasn't certain. He could tell Janie he tried to help the great Erin Carlile. Surely, she'd appreciate that much since he couldn't ask them to stop by city hall to meet an adoring fan. Not if they were in a hurry to get back to Boston. "Thanks for checking, Chloe."

"Wait!" He heard shuffling and something metallic like a dog bowl crash. "I have one bag left. Have them swing by here."

"I'll send them over." He ended the call and faced the woman who, though she didn't know it, had the power to help Janie realize all her greatest dreams. "My sister has one bag left." He gave them the address, which Erin quickly typed into her phone.

"You've literally saved Christmas," Erin said. "Is there any way we can repay you for the favor?"

Will's automatic response was *no*, because his kindness was never extended with an ulterior motive. But this was about more than him. This was the woman he loved and the dream that meant everything to her. "Actually, my best friend is a huge fan of your work. She's always wanted to attend one of your galas." Will was proud of himself for remembering the correct terminology, though he'd heard Janie use it enough times. "If you ever have spare tickets to an event, could you please consider adding her to the guest list?"

"I'd be happy to."

Digging through his wallet, Will found one of Janie's cards. She'd kill him if she found out he'd given one of these old business cards to her idol since she'd been talking nonstop about updating them with her new and improved event planner image. But her phone number was the same, and that's what mattered. "Thank you."

"Thank *you*."

Will watched as Erin and her husband navigated to the front door, but instead of feeling excited that he'd just possibly secured the best Christmas present ever for his best friend, he felt restless. Was there something more he was supposed to do?

The First Annual Snowy Falls Christmas Eve Charity Event tickets fell out of his pocket again and dropped to the floor. He stared at the shiny red admittance tickets until it dawned on him. *Of course, there's something more to do, Will.* It wasn't enough that Janie might someday get a call about tickets to some gala. A *maybe* wasn't a gift at all.

The bells about the door clamored as it fell shut behind the departing couple. It hit Will that unless he went now, he might never see them again. In an effort to rush after them, he slipped on the hardwood floor but caught himself on an endcap and ran outside. "Wait!" he called after Erin and her husband.

They turned, their expression a mixture of curious and slightly annoyed. "I know you live in Boston," he said counting out three tickets and offering them up. "But if you were looking for something different to do with the family on Christmas Eve, you should come back to Snowy Falls. Janie Arden, the friend I mentioned, it's her event."

Much to his surprise, Erin smiled warmly as she accepted the tickets. Will expected her to scoff at them or produce a vague excuse about why they couldn't attend. Instead, Erin glanced at her husband and said, "I have a rare holiday off from planning. We were talking about doing something more family-friendly this year."

"Caroline would love reindeer bingo," Erin's husband said to her. "And the gingerbread house competition. She's been begging to enter one ever since she watched that movie."

"It's all she talks about," Erin said to Will. "Thank you for the tickets. We'll definitely keep this in mind."

Will watched as Erin hurried to her car and drove off with her husband, not sure whether to feel excitement or dread. Janie would be over the moon if Erin showed up tomorrow. *That* would be the best gift he could ever give her. But his kind gesture might be the very reason Janie took off for Boston before he even had time to submit his official application for the Snowy Falls deputy fire chief position.

He would never stand in the way of her dreams, even if it meant giving up on his own. But after the best kiss of his life, he hated to think of a future that didn't include Janie Arden by his side.

## CHAPTER 10

# JANIE

"You don't have to help us with the food, Janie," Mom said for what had to be the third time since she'd come by the restaurant—maybe the fourth. She'd lost count.

Her parents closed The Twisted Lobster after the lunch rush so they could focus on preparing the catering order for tomorrow's event. They, along with a couple of staff members, had been working nonstop since they locked the doors. But with the second round of printed tickets all sold, Janie had stopped by to request more food than originally planned. The least she could do was lend them a hand. It had nothing to do with avoiding Will Taggert.

"The auditorium is decorated to the nines, all the tickets are sold, and everything is a go for tomorrow." Janie took the wooden spoon from Mom and used it to stir the homemade pasta. If she lived to be a hundred, she doubted she'd ever find pasta as wonderful as the century-old family recipe. "I have time to help with the food since the order doubled, so let me help."

"What about Will?" Mom pressed.

The spoon slipped from Janie's grip and dropped into the large pot. She barely retrieved it before it sank completely into the boiling water, and not without scorching her fingertips. "What about him?" Janie asked, wrapping her hand in her apron to wipe away the steam and tamp down the sting.

"What's he doing now that you're all caught up on event planning?" Mom's question might sound innocent to someone who didn't know better, but Janie did. *Not you too.* "Maybe he'd be able to help? As you mentioned, it *is* a rather large order."

"He probably has family stuff," she answered without lifting her gaze from the pasta. She'd kept busy all day, careful not to allow a moment alone with her best friend as they decorated the auditorium and set up the many different stations and booths. Always having an audience meant they couldn't talk about that kiss.

Though Janie very much wanted another, her plan had worked. She refused to complicate things and potentially stand in the way of Will's promotion. Having known him for well over a decade, she knew he'd selflessly set aside his own desires if it meant making her happy. She decided the only fair thing to do was pretend as if that kiss meant nothing. *Blame it on the mistletoe.*

"Is everything okay between you two?" Mom asked.

"Of course."

She felt Mom's assessing gaze even though she refused to meet it head on. "Are you sure? It's just that you're here tonight of all nights—"

"It's Christmas Eve Eve," Janie said with a shrug. "What's so special about that?"

"It's the night before your biggest event. Shouldn't you be doing something fun, or at least relaxing? I'm surprised Will isn't pounding at the door, demanding you come with him. He always seems to know when you've worked too hard and need a well-deserved break."

Now that Mom mentioned it, it *did* feel odd. Will was always there to make sure she didn't over-work herself or that she remembered to eat. He'd been just as distant with her today as she'd been with him. How had she not noticed until now? "I told you. He has family stuff. I'll see him tomorrow, Mom."

Mom grabbed her by both shoulders and

squeezed. "I just don't want you taking the time you have left here for granted."

"The time I have left?"

"Before you move to Boston." It felt like a lifetime ago that Janie proclaimed her intentions to stay single and put all her energy into her event planning business so she could set up shop in Boston. Had it really only been a few days? "You *are* still moving to Boston, aren't you?"

"Of course. As soon as I can figure out how to make it all work."

Mom looked across the room at Dad, and they shared a knowing smile. Her parents had an unspoken language all their own. It was one of the many reasons Janie not only admired their relationship, but set the bar so high for her own. At least, she always thought that was the reason none of her holiday boyfriends lasted.

*Unless . . .*

"We were going to wait until Christmas," Dad said, wiping his hands on a towel.

"For what?" Janie asked.

Mom steered Janie toward the empty dining room with a firm but loving hand on her shoulder. "We want to give you your present early."

Janie's eyebrows drew together. "I thought we agreed no gifts this year." It'd been her idea when she stole a glance at the books a couple of weeks ago. The restaurant was in the black, but barely. Janie had cheated and bought her parents gifts anyway, but they weren't supposed to spend a dime on her.

"You really thought we'd listen?" Mom teased.

Dad brought his hand out from behind his back and offered an envelope to her. "We want you to know how proud we are of you. Everyone in town has nothing but high praises about your abilities to put together heartfelt events."

Janie stared at the sealed envelope, wondering if they'd gifted her a day at the new spa down the street. She could use a deep tissue massage after all the running around and heavy lifting these past few days. But why the gift couldn't wait until Christmas—

"It's true," Mom added, adoration twinkling in her eyes. "Every volunteer we've fed has gone on and on about the miracle you pulled off with the charity event. You have a real gift. You've spent years helping us with the restaurant. Now we want to help *you* follow your dream."

"Merry Christmas, Janie," Dad said.

Both parents watched her open the envelope, their excited grins barely containable as Janie pulled out a check. Her eyes doubled in size at the amount. "Did you guys rob a bank or something?" she asked with a nervous laugh.

"Don't be silly, Janie," Mom said, dropping her hand back to Janie's shoulder. "We've been saving this all year."

"But how? I—I saw the books. You're barely making ends meet. You can't afford this."

"The restaurant has had its best year ever," Dad explained. "When you were snooping through the books, you must've missed the large monthly transfers. We left just enough in the operating account to keep things running comfortably and saved the rest."

"We want you to chase your dreams, sweetie," Mom added.

Janie's pulse quickened as happy tears sprang to her eyes. The large lump sum would be more than enough to rent an office space in Boston, build a professional website, and buy all the supplies she would need. She might even be able to spring for a part-time assistant. "I don't know what to say."

Both her parents enveloped her in a bear hug, squeezing the air right out of her lungs.

"We even have a friend in Boston who can help you find an office," Dad added, finally releasing his tight grip and allowing air back into her lungs. "You can start looking right after Christmas if you want."

The first urge she had was to call Will and beg him to come to Boston with her the day after Christmas to start looking at office spaces. But when she remembered she couldn't ask him to move with her, her stomach knotted. Could they make the long-distance thing work? Snowy Falls was only an hour—maybe two on a bad traffic day—away. It could work for the short term. But long term?

"Janie's speechless," Mom said to Dad. "Mark *this* on your calendar and circle it with a bright red marker."

"Chef Arden?" one of the staff called from the doorway. "We need your help with the sauce."

"Duty calls," Dad said, disappearing through the kitchen door.

"Mom, are you *sure* you guys can afford this?" Janie asked, needing to hear once more that her parents wouldn't go bankrupt from their generous offering.

"Yes, sweetie. We planned this last Christmas. We could tell you were about done dating those throwaway boyfriends that distracted you from your own dreams. We had a feeling a fire would be lit under you this year, and we were right. Look at you stepping up to take over planning the biggest Christmas event Snowy Falls has ever seen. And in only a few days!" Mom squeezed her in a side hug. "I *am* going to miss you, though."

"I'm only going to be an hour away. I'll be in Snowy Falls all the time."

"No, you won't." Mom adjusted her apron, preparing to return to the kitchen. "I know you think you will. But once you're in Boston, you'll be busier than you expect establishing your new life." Mom must've noticed Janie's fallen expression. "It's okay, sweetie. It's part of pursuing your own happiness. We want you to realize all your wildest dreams. I also want you to have realistic expectations." A clamoring of pots drew Mom's attention. "I better see what's happening in there."

Janie sank into a chair, staring at the check.

She should feel elated and on the verge of screaming in excitement. The only thing this check *didn't* do was make valuable connections she'd need to be hired for the galas and banquets she wanted most to plan. But Janie could build those over time. She could leave the day after Christmas if she wanted and start building her lifelong dream in Boston.

So why wasn't she happier?

# JANIE

"If I didn't know any better, I'd say you found a little bit of Christmas magic to pull this all off," Grandma Annie said to Janie while she waited in line at the photo booth. Of all the stations set up, the photo booth was by far the most popular. Second only to Santa and his helper, Grimm, of course. The kids couldn't get enough of the dynamic duo.

"I don't think there's any other way to explain how we brought this all together in time," Janie agreed. "I'm so glad you decided to take a break from cooking and came out."

"Once I saw there was reindeer bingo on the

agenda, I couldn't stay away." Grandma Annie patted her purse. "I didn't win the jackpot at the main event, you see. It was someone else's turn this year. But I *have* won three rounds and fifty bucks today."

"Wow, that's amazing."

"Plus, Blakely's watching the roast and peeling potatoes until I get back to the house. Under the watchful eye of Everly. Can't have that girl running off to Cancun again this year."

Will, disguised as the most handsome Santa Janie had ever seen, looked up from his post across the room and locked eyes with her. His fluffy white beard hid his lips, but she caught the smile dancing in his eyes. Her heart soared, until she remembered her dilemma.

"Everything all right, dear?" Grandma Annie asked.

"Actually—"

"Janie Arden, this is amazing!" Lynette Jergensen grabbed on to Janie's elbow and refused to let go. "I can't believe you pulled this off in just a few short days. I heard about all the vendors who canceled on you last minute. It's a wonder we have an event at all."

"Good thing they bailed," Grandma Annie said. "The old event was too stuffy for this town. Janie gave it a much-needed facelift, and look how great it turned out. Practically every person in town is here."

"It *is* great. We've already raised twice our goal for the homeless shelter," Lynette added, finally dropping her hand. "Just think of how many families in need our community will be helping this holiday season."

One had to only look around the auditorium to see how great a success The First Annual Snowy Falls Christmas Eve Charity Event had turned out to be. Every station had lines. Her parents were packing up warmers as most of the food was gone. And mountains of gifts sat around the designated tree for the toy drive.

Janie felt a sort of glow radiate through her that she could only describe as a mixture of pride and appreciation at being a part of something so special. In her hometown of all places. It was a feeling she never expected to experience until she moved to Boston.

"I hope you'll volunteer to plan next year's event," Lynette asked. "And every year after that."

"I—"

"Oh, excuse me. My husband is waving me over," Lynette said, seemingly oblivious to Janie's potential hiccup in that plan. If she were in Boston, she would most certainly be booked over the holidays and unable to head the event here in town. "Merry Christmas, ladies."

"Janie Arden?" someone called.

Grandma Annie patted her arm. "If you have

any energy left after the Christmas Eve tree lighting tonight, tell Will to bring you along to my place for dinner. You're practically family already." She slipped away much quicker than a woman of her years should be able, leaving Janie's heart racing. Was Grandma Annie implying Janie should come with Will as his friend or his date?

Will sent her a quick wave and a smile that his beard couldn't hide. Butterflies erupted in her stomach. Dozens. Maybe hundreds. *This is problematic.*

"Excuse me, are you Janie Arden?"

Janie spun around toward the unfamiliar female voice and almost screamed. Standing before her was the woman and legend, Erin Carlile. Dizziness threatened to knock Janie flat on her back, but she gripped the cold metal edge of a round table to steady herself. "You're—you're Erin—"

"Erin Carlile." She extended her hand. "I hear you're the mastermind behind this festive event."

Discreetly, Janie pinched her forearm. She probably shouldn't wake herself from the insane dream, but on the one percent chance that it was reality, she didn't want to risk a bad first impression with her idol. She may not get another chance. "Yes, I am."

"I also heard that you had to recreate the whole thing in three days."

Janie's eyebrows drew in confusion, wondering how long Erin had been wandering the auditorium and how many locals she'd chatted with to find out that piece of information. Grandma Annie was the most likely candidate to freely divulge that information to a stranger, but she'd been talking to Janie that whole time. "We event planners run in small circles here in New England. Vanessa Blake is a friend of mine."

"Is she okay?" Janie asked, remembering the mention of a skiing accident.

"Two cracked ribs and a broken leg. But after the tumble she took down a double black diamond trail, she's lucky to be alive." Erin scanned the room, her gaze seemingly taking in every inch from floor to ceiling to the gossamer and white Christmas lights draped overhead. "She'd be stunned at the miracle you pulled off. She feels just awful about everyone who canceled on you, but seems it was for the best."

"Snowy Falls is more of a family-friendly town," Janie said honestly.

"You have a knack."

Janie glanced over her shoulder at Will, but he wasn't in his assigned seat. Nor was Grimm. Santa's helper likely needed a quick break outside after all the cookies the kids had been feeding him. "Thank you for saying so."

"I don't say things I don't mean."

"Can I ask you something?"

"Of course."

"How do you do it all?" Janie asked. "I'm a big fan of your work. I've never been lucky enough to attend one of your events, but I've followed them through blogs, articles, and reviews. You're like superwoman."

Erin glanced over Janie's shoulder, her lips curling into a warm smile. When Janie followed that gaze, she spotted a tall man in jeans and a sweater with a hand draped over the shoulder of a little girl. "I don't do it all alone," Erin admitted. "Without Theo, I would never have made it as far as I did. When I was first starting out, I used to beg him to help me carry heavy boxes up flights of stairs. He's been my rock."

ILL

"Grimm, c'mon," Will called to the dog who was shirking his elf duties by staring intently up a tree. A squirrel taunted him from one of the highest branches, eliciting a few whimpers from the dog. "We need to get back inside. The kids are waiting. It's not my fault you let them know you can high five."

But as much as he loved them, it wasn't the kids Will was most eager to see.

It was Janie.

All day long they'd been sneaking glances and sharing secret smiles from across the room. Yesterday, he'd been convinced all was lost since Janie went out of her way to avoid him. But if he was being honest with himself, he'd been avoiding her, too. He was afraid her idol would show up today and offer her everything she ever wanted.

The selfish part of him hoped the prestigious event planner from Boston had better things to do than drive all the way back to little Snowy Falls for a small-town Christmas event. But the selfless part of him that only wanted Janie to live out her wildest dreams was relieved Erin Carlile showed up and introduced herself to Janie.

It didn't mean he could stand witnessing the joyous moment that might very well mean the end of a relationship he and Janie never had a chance to pursue. Everyone in town was raving about the miracle she pulled off in record time. The turnout alone testified to its success. Erin Carlile would be a fool to dismiss her talents.

"C'mon, Grimm."

"Is that one of your reindeer, Santa?" an eager-eyed kid, maybe four or five, asked, reminding Will he was still fully decked out in costume.

Grimm stood taller, as if he knew the little boy was talking about him.

"Sure is."

"Where are his antlers?"

Will shared a kind smile with the boy's parents. "He's not very good about keeping them on."

"Can he fly?"

"Not without his antlers." Will held the door open for the family as Grimm snuck a lick to the kid's cheek. The little boy giggled in delight. The family passed through the hall and headed for the propped-open double doors, handing tickets to the women at the front.

As much as Will loved the people of Snowy Falls, he wasn't quite ready to dive head-first back into the chaos. He urged Grimm down a narrow hall that circled half the auditorium. It was easier to slip back to his spot this way so he didn't risk the Great Dane's whipping tail knocking anything over. Plus, it was a nearly deserted path of least resistance when it came to women like Alicia Meadows who were still hot on his tail.

"I could use an event planner on staff who understands small towns. Someone who can really capture the essence and deliver events like this one on demand." He recognized the woman's voice even though he couldn't see around the corner. Will yanked Grimm's leash to a halt, hoping the dog hadn't given them away with his click-clacking claws.

"You're offering me a job?" Janie asked, a mixture of surprise and exhilaration in a tone he'd grown to know so well over the years. He could practically feel her bubbly excitement wrapping him in one of her deliriously happy hugs.

"I'd need you to start right away." Will heard a zipper but didn't dare peek around the corner to see what was happening. If Janie saw him, she might be tempted to think about the offer rather than jump on it. "Here."

"Are these—"

"Two tickets to the New Year's Eve gala I'm planning. It's the fanciest event of the season. Do you have an evening gown?"

"Yes!"

"Make sure you bring a date who wears a tux. The dress code is strictly enforced."

"Of course. I'm sure I can find one in time."

Will's stomach twisted in an uncomfortable knot as he was taken back to the city council meeting, to the conversation where Janie laughed at him when he offered to be her date to a fancy event. It was true that he'd only ever wore a tux to his siblings' weddings—and only ones he'd rented. Though he would gladly suffer through a gala in the most uncomfortable tuxedo for Janie's sake, she would always see his disdain for the formal attire as a wedge between them. A distinct difference in what each of them wanted out of life. Maybe *this* was the sign he'd been ignoring all along.

"I'll need you to come to Boston right after Christmas. I have a backlog of work—unless you're afraid of long days?"

"They're the only kind I know."

"Good to hear. I look forward to having you on board, Janie Arden."

Will stumbled backward, dragging Grimm with him before the dog gave them away with one of his famous whines. He was confused why they were running *away* from their friend, but Will needed to get away much worse than the town needed a Santa and his goofy helper.

## CHAPTER 13

ANIE

Janie spun in a complete circle, searching the auditorium for a man in a red suit. But Santa was nowhere to be found. "How much water did Grimm drink?" she mumbled to herself.

"Looking for something?" Libby, Will's middle sister, asked.

"Will. Have you seen him?" Janie's heart still raced from the unbelievable conversation in the hallway with Erin Carlile. The only person she wanted to talk to about it right now was Will Taggert.

"Sorry, I only just got here a few minutes ago.

I've been working all morning, and I'm starved." It was now that Janie noticed Libby still wore her dark green apron adorned with paw prints and a smattering of dog hair. She looked positively exhausted, but the sparkle in her eyes was undeniable. It was the look of hard work and satisfaction from pursuing her passion. One Janie realized she *already* knew well.

The event planner Janie'd admired for years offered to hire her. It was more than she ever dreamed possible. Except, it wasn't *her* dream.

Yes, fancy galas and banquets would be exciting to plan. But it was Erin's personal compliment earlier that made Janie realize how much she truly loved capturing the essence of small towns in each and every one of her events. She'd been taking those smaller events for granted for so long, she'd almost given them up completely. It wasn't just the challenge that fueled her passion, but the heartfelt charm she imbued into every single one.

"Please tell me the lobster mac and cheese isn't all gone?" Libby asked.

"I think it's the only thing left. But you better hurry."

"Oh, good!" Libby took two quick steps forward, then stopped. "Wait, was Will"—she looked around her and lowered her voice, likely for the sake of tiny ears—"Santa?"

"Yeah."

"I *did* see a man in a red suit headed down the

block. My guess is that he went to the fire station." Libby glanced at the serving table, then back to Janie. "Everything all right with you two?"

Janie's heart squeezed with hope. "I think it will be. If I can just *find* your brother first."

"I want to see Santa!" Janie heard a little boy cry. She tried to offer an apologetic look to the boy's mother, but she was too busy consoling the sobbing kid. Janie needed to bring Santa back not only for her sake, but for the sake of the kiddos eagerly waiting their turn to meet him.

"Get some food. I'm going to rescue Santa before we have a full-fledged holiday meltdown in here." Janie grabbed her purse but left her coat. There wasn't time to shrug it on or fiddle with the pesky zipper. What she had to tell him couldn't wait.

Outside city hall, she searched up and down the block but the light, puffy snowflakes quickly covered new tracks. She could only hope that Libby was right about the fire station. Perhaps Will was there now, filling out an application. Though why he'd leave the event without a word was a mystery.

She hurried down the block, searching the snow-covered sidewalks for hints of massive paw prints. But the giant snowflakes buried all clues.

At the fire station, Janie yanked on the cold metal door handle. The door rattled against her efforts but didn't budge. She could see a faint glow from a hall light that never turned off, but no sign of Will or anyone else inside.

"Will, where are you?" she muttered to no one.

She heard jingling before she caught sight of its cause. Every shop in Snowy Falls was closed, and almost everyone was either at the charity event or at home taking a nap to recover from the first string of festivities. The metallic tinkling echoed across the empty street, and Janie listened intently to identify the source.

"Where—"

A gust of wind nearly knocked her over as a giant beast charged down the sidewalk past her.

"Grimm?"

The Great Dane let out an enthusiastic bark as his green bandana came loose and floated to her. She caught it before a gust of wind yanked it across the street.

"Grimm, come back!" she called as she ran after the dog, turning down the block from the downtown strip into a residential neighborhood. But her kitten-heeled boots weren't made for running on slick sidewalks or sprinting through snowy yards. "Grimm, I'm going to tell Santa to put you on his naughty—"

Janie ran head first into a solid something and flew backward.

## CHAPTER 14

ANIE

Janie had only half a second to register the woodsy cologne mixed with a hint of peppermint before she tumbled into a snowbank.

"Janie?" She could hear Will's voice, but when she attempted to open her eyes, all she saw was black. No, that wasn't quite right. It was more a dark blue and cold. *Like snow.* She was staring at a wall of snow. "Janie, are you okay?"

She spit out snowflakes as he tugged her upright. But her legs, tired from running in shoes not fit for such activities, gave out. She plopped back into the snowbank, accidentally pulling Will with her. Or had Grimm run past them and not-so-accidentally given Will a nudge?

They laughed as they both struggled to sitting positions.

"Where have you been, *Santa*?" Janie demanded playfully, not minding one bit that Will had shed the beard. She liked his own two-day-old stubble so much better than that fake fluffy white concoction. "Some of the kids are minutes from naughty-list tantrums." Her tone didn't match the urgency of her words. In fact, she didn't feel much urgency at all to get back despite her shivering. "I've been looking for you, you know."

"I needed some air. Why aren't you wearing a coat?" He draped an arm around her, snuggling her against his warm body. "I'd offer you mine, but it's attached to the rest of the suit."

"I didn't have time to grab my coat because I was looking for *you*."

"I told you. Just needed some air."

Will's melancholy tone caused her to study his expression closer. His forced smile didn't fool her one bit. "The one thing we've never been able to do is lie to each other," she said, unsurprised when her gaze dropped to his lips. She could reach her fingers to his chin and turn his face toward hers. Was a kiss in a snowbank romantic? She definitely wanted to find out.

"I saw that you met Erin Carlile. Congratu-lations."

"Congratulations?" She looked at him like he'd grown two heads. "That's a weird thing to say about meeting someone."

"I heard she offered you your dream job. It's everything you've ever wanted." He brushed the snow from his knees and pushed up to his feet. He reached a hand out for Janie. "You'll be leaving soon, won't you?"

Janie stared at the outstretched hand, reached for it, and yanked him back down in the snow.

Will patted at his red pants even harder, his annoyance shining through. "Janie, this isn't funny."

Grimm's enthusiastic bark and frolic through the snow around them said otherwise. "I'm not leaving at all."

Will stopped mid-brush and stared at her. "What do you mean you're not leaving? Of course, you're leaving. Right after Christmas. Isn't that what she said?"

"Yeah, it's what she said." Janie was stunned by Erin Carlile's instant job offer. She'd been so caught up in the moment she *almost* said yes without thinking it through. Had it been a week ago, the answer would've been a no-brainer. But it was Erin's own admission about her husband supporting her every step of the way that really hit home for Janie.

"Are you staying long enough to finish planning the holiday parties you already promised to do?"

Janie shifted in the snow to better face Will, ignoring the cold soaking her pantlegs as long as she could. "Have I ever thanked you for all the times you've dropped everything to help me? For all those times I begged you to carry the heavy boxes when the elevator was out? I've made you listen to hundreds of hours of ideas, and never once did you complain."

"That's what friends are for, Janie. They're there for each other."

"True," she admitted as Grimm plopped down in the snow beside them, dropping his head in Will's lap, demanding head scratches. "But all that seems a little beyond the call of friendship. I only wish I'd figured it out sooner."

Will dared a glance at her. "Figured *what* out sooner?"

She let out an exaggerated sigh and added a playful roll of her eyes. He was her best friend and had been since elementary school. Odds were he knew exactly what she was about to say, only he was making her work for it. "You're going to make me come out and say it, aren't you?"

Will reached for her hand, squeezing it with his own. "Before you say anything, I need to say something first."

"What happened to ladies first?" she teased.

"I love you, Janie. I have since the sixth grade."

The admission, though one she'd hoped for, shocked her to the core. "Since *sixth* grade?" She remembered her conversation with Chloe about Will not dating for longer than they could remember. Had he been waiting all this time for her to figure out her feelings for him? It seemed a stretch.

"Yes, Janie Arden. I've been hopelessly pining after you for an embarrassing number of years." He cupped her cheek, his chilly fingers heating instantly against her warm cheek. "But I don't want you to stay in Snowy Falls and give up your dream to make this work. That isn't fair to you. And as much as I love you—" Grimm nudged him so hard he nearly bumped heads with Janie. "As much as *we* love you, we can't move to Boston."

"I know. You'd never be happy there. Either of you, because your home is here."

He caressed her cheek as Grimm looked up at both of them, making it hard to focus on words. "That's why I would never ask you to go."

"And I can't ask you to stay."

"But you didn't. I *chose* to stay."

Will looked at her, confusion dancing in his deep brown eyes. "But Erin—"

"She offered me a chance to work *for* her. Though it would be a life-changing opportunity, it still means I wouldn't be my own boss. My dream is to run my own successful event planning business."

"But the fancy banquets—"

"If there's one thing I learned from taking over the Christmas Eve event here in Snowy Falls, it's that *fancy* is not really my style. I mean, it might be fun to dress up and attend a real gala. Since Erin gave me tickets, I'm so getting you in a tuxedo for New Year's Eve." Janie reached for Will's cheek, tugging him toward her until their foreheads rested against one another.

"Good luck."

"Oh, it's happening."

"You really think you'll be happy without galas and all that?"

"Those events, stunning as they are, aren't the ones I want to build my legacy around. Not anymore. I'm good at the smaller, more meaningful ones. It's a calling I've been denying, but no more. I want to create special events people will remember for years to come. I made a very valuable connection with Erin Carlile. One that will help jumpstart my dream in a big way. But I want my home base to be right here, in Snowy Falls. With the man—and dog— I love beside me."

"You *love* me?"

"Of course, I do." She lifted her chin, closing the gap between their lips. The kiss warmed her from the inside out, making her forget they were sitting in a snowbank or that she was missing her coat. "I love you very much, Will Taggert. I'm only sorry it took me so long to realize it."

"Better late than never." He brought their lips together again, and she melted against him as the kiss deepened. Seemed that Santa knew what she needed for Christmas better than she did, and she couldn't be happier for the best gift she could ever receive.

ONE YEAR LATER . . .

WILL

"Ready to go?" Will asked, closing the glass door behind him as sleigh bells jingled overhead. Grimm trotted across the open office space, his whipping tail lifting flyers from a coffee table as snowflakes flew from his coat and melted midair. The charming space one block from city hall in Snowy Falls was everything Janie ever dreamed it would be, all thanks to her parents generous Christmas gift last year.

"Hey, buddy." Janie hugged Grimm's giant head against her chest, her resilient gaze lifting to meet Will's. He was the luckiest man alive to have a wife who looked at him that way. "I'm almost done here."

Will dropped into a cushioned chair beside her

desk and let out a yawn. They'd been working nonstop to make The Second Annual Snowy Falls Christmas Eve Charity Event even better than the first. Between that and his duties as deputy fire chief, he was ready to take his wife home and snuggle on the couch for the rest of the evening. The event would keep them plenty busy tomorrow. "The decorations are all up and ready for your final approval. Then we can grab dinner and head home."

"I swear your mom cleaned out her entire attic this year," Janie said, scribbling one last note before closing her planner.

"She did. But only so she had an excuse to add even more Christmas decorations to her collection. As long as we live in Snowy Falls, you'll never have to worry about where to get holiday décor for any of your events."

"That's good because I just added two more January Christmas parties to the books."

"I thought we agreed you'd start slowing down," Will said, his tone lovingly firm. "The further along—"

"Say, I saw Libby with some guy earlier today," Janie cut in. "They were walking down the street away from me, so I didn't get a good look at him. But he doesn't look like he's from around here. Any idea who he is?"

"A guy?" Will shook his head, allowing Janie to change the subject because they both already knew he'd never let her work too many hours when she needed rest the most. "I think the whole Taggert clan would know if she was dating someone, if that's what you're implying. It's not exactly something our family can keep secret from one another."

Janie pushed out of her chair, using the desk to help lift her up before Will could hop out of his seat to help her. Her swollen belly was growing every day, but she was still quicker getting around than he could predict. Soon, Noah and Everly's daughter would have a cousin. He imagined Grandma Annie's Christmas Eve feast was only going to grow more crowded each Christmas.

"She's been kicking today."

"You mean *he's* been kicking."

Janie playfully rolled her eyes. "Don't get your hopes up. My mom swears that every generation in our family for decades has started off with a girl."

Will slid his hand onto her cheek, bringing their foreheads together. "You just want a mini event planner at your side."

"She can be a firefighter, too. I'm open minded." She tilted her head up and stole the kiss Will had been thinking about all day. As it did every time, the brush of her lips sent electricity zinging throughout his body and made the world around them disappear.

It was only a knock on the storefront window that tugged Will back to reality. They looked over to see Chloe and Parker waving at them. Belle pressed her nose against the window, causing Grimm to dart to the glass. The two did a dance as Will helped Janie into her coat. "No way I'm letting you go outside without a coat, *mama*."

She snaked her hand up his neck and stole another kiss. "Have I told you how much I love you today, Will Taggert?"

"I can't remember. You better tell me again just in case."

## SWEET ROMANCE

Sunset Ridge Series
    1 - Moose Be Love
    2 - My Favorite Moosetake
    3 - Annoymoosely Yours
    4 - Love & Moosechief
    5 - Under the Mooseltoe
    6 - Moosely Over You
    7 - Absomoosely in Love

Starlight Cowboys Series
    1 - Cowboys & Starlight
    2 - Cowboys & Firelight
    3 - Cowboys & Sunrises
    4 - Cowboys & Moonlight
    5 - Cowboys & Mistletoe

6 - Cowboys & Shooting Stars

Stand-Alone
    *Hooked on You

Christmas in Snowy Falls
    1 - Pawsitively in Love Again at Christmas
    2 - Pawsitively Home for Christmas
    3 - Pawsitively Yours for Christmas

————

## STEAMY ROMANTIC SUSPENSE

Willow Creek Series
    1 - Sweetly Scandalous
    2 - Secretly Scandalous
    3 - Simply Scandalous

Sign up for Jacqueline Winter's newsletter to receive alerts about current projects and new releases!

http://eepurl.com/du18iz

# ABOUT THE AUTHOR

Jacqueline Winters has been writing since she was nine when she'd sneak stacks of paper from her grandma's closet and fill them with adventure. She grew up in small-town Nebraska and spent a decade living in beautiful Alaska. She writes sweet contemporary romance and contemporary romantic suspense.

She's a sucker for happily ever after's, has a sweet tooth that can be sated with cupcakes. On a relaxing evening, you can find her at her computer writing her next novel with her faithful dog poking his adorable nose over her keyboard.

www.ingramcontent.com/pod-product-compliance
Lightning Source LLC
Chambersburg PA
CBHW031331160726
47993CB00002B/621